Knitting & Starlight

De-ann Black

Text copyright © 2024 by De-ann Black
Cover Design & Illustration © 2024 by De-ann Black

All rights reserved.
No part of this book may be used or reproduced in any manner whatsoever without the written consent of the author.

This is a work of fiction. Names, characters, places, and incidents are either products of the author's imagination or are used fictitiously. Any resemblance to actual persons, living or dead, businesses, companies, events, or locales is entirely coincidental.

Paperback edition published 2024

Knitting & Starlight

ISBN: 9798329188264

Knitting & Starlight is the second book in the Music, Dance & Romance series.

1. The Sweetest Waltz
2. Knitting & Starlight

Also by De-ann Black (Romance, Action/Thrillers & Children's books). See her Amazon Author page or website for further details about her books, screenplays, illustrations and artwork. www.De-annBlack.com

Romance:
Knitting Bee
The Sweetest Waltz
Sweet Music
Love & Lyrics
Christmas Weddings
Fairytale Christmas on the Island
The Cure for Love at Christmas
Vintage Dress Shop on the Island
Scottish Island Fairytale Castle
Scottish Loch Summer Romance
Scottish Island Knitting Bee
Sewing & Mending Cottage
Knitting Shop by the Sea
Colouring Book Cottage
Knitting Cottage
Oops! I'm the Paparazzi, Again
The Bitch-Proof Wedding
Embroidery Cottage
The Dressmaker's Cottage
The Sewing Shop
Heather Park
The Tea Shop by the Sea
The Bookshop by the Seaside
The Sewing Bee
The Quilting Bee
Snow Bells Wedding
Snow Bells Christmas
Summer Sewing Bee
The Chocolatier's Cottage
Christmas Cake Chateau

The Beemaster's Cottage
The Sewing Bee By The Sea
The Flower Hunter's Cottage
The Christmas Knitting Bee
The Sewing Bee & Afternoon Tea
Shed In The City
The Bakery By The Seaside
The Christmas Chocolatier
The Christmas Tea Shop & Bakery
The Bitch-Proof Suit

Action/Thrillers:
Knight in Miami.
Agency Agenda.
Love Him Forever.
Someone Worse.
Electric Shadows.
The Strife of Riley.
Shadows of Murder.

Colouring books:
Summer Nature. Flower Nature. Summer Garden. Spring Garden. Autumn Garden. Sea Dream. Festive Christmas. Christmas Garden. Flower Bee. Wild Garden. Flower Hunter. Stargazer Space. Christmas Theme. Faerie Garden Spring. Scottish Garden Seasons. Bee Garden.

Embroidery books:
Floral Garden Embroidery Patterns
Floral Spring Embroidery Patterns
Christmas & Winter Embroidery Patterns
Floral Nature Embroidery Designs
Scottish Garden Embroidery Designs

Contents

Chapter One	1
Chapter Two	14
Chapter Three	35
Chapter Four	48
Chapter Five	63
Chapter Six	76
Chapter Seven	90
Chapter Eight	104
Chapter Nine	115
Chapter Ten	129
Chapter Eleven	144
Chapter Twelve	158
Chapter Thirteen	174
Chapter Fourteen	183
Chapter Fifteen	197
About De-ann Black	228

CHAPTER ONE

Edinburgh wore autumn well.

Burnished gold and bronze tones of the trees and greenery in the heart of the Scottish city enhanced the classic architecture. Everything from the historic spires reaching up into the golden glow of the morning sky, to the traditional buildings from past eras, suited the new season.

The city had looked beautiful in the summer, but upped its game in the autumn. The colours were gorgeous.

Mari wore autumn unintentionally.

Dressed in a marigold yellow jumper, that matched the full name she rarely used, and a chestnut cardigan jacket, both garments she'd knitted herself, she'd teamed them with taupe ankle boots and slim–fitting cinnamon cords that flattered her slender but shapely figure.

A strawberry blonde, thirty, with a pale complexion, and green eyes that viewed the world with curiosity, she walked along the narrow cobbled street.

Impressive architecture rose up on both sides of the winding street where an eclectic mix of shops and eateries were nestled into the old–world buildings.

Narrow alleyways, closes and stairways trailed off from the cobbled thoroughfare.

The heart of it interlocked, winding and twirling around until it met up with itself again. It wasn't giving anyone the runaround, just a tour in shadows and light to intrigue the senses.

Mari had popped out to the nearby grocery shop to buy fresh bread and milk for her breakfast. The world around her had blinked awake an hour before she ventured out of the tiny flat she rented above a craft shop, but was still stretching into life. It was such a lovely autumn morning that she went for a short stroll after buying her groceries, meandering where the cobbled street led her.

Vaguely familiar with the local landscape, a few hidden gems had continued to reveal themselves, like the one she now saw across from her. A theatre?

She frowned against the golden sunlight. There was a theatre hiding in plain sight! She'd never noticed it before, and walked over for a closer look. She spent a fair share of her earnings and time going to shows throughout the city. It was a perk and a privilege of living there.

But this little theatre felt like finding a treasure trove of untapped entertainment, almost on her doorstep. How handy.

It was only when she went over that she saw there was a notice pinned to the inside of the window at the side of the front entrance. The entrance itself could be easily missed as the whole facia blended into the old–fashioned architecture.

Mari read the notice. It was handwritten in an ornate cursive style that just missed being calligraphy. Classy, she thought, and then her heart jolted as she took in the message:

Stage plays wanted. Must be original. Never before performed.

She blinked and reread it. Submissions were wanted! The details of where to send the submissions was nothing more than the theatre's email address. No person in particular. Just send it and wing it.

Her heart picked up pace. She loved knitting, tholed her aptitude for doing accounts, but what she'd always dreamed of was writing plays and having them performed in the theatre.

Snapping a copy of the notice with her phone, she scurried away before anyone saw her. She needed to think this through. Dare she submit the new play she'd been working on recently? The third and a half one she'd written with a serious view to having them performed.

Maybe.

Her heart still alight with hope and trepidation, she wound her way back to where she was living above a little craft shop, thinking about the theatre and pondering whether to submit her new play, *The Shop That Sells Everything*, to them.

Since leaving her job at the accountancy firm, she didn't need to watch the clock, and made her own hours. Working for herself for less than one season, independence still felt shaky, but she was determined to give it a go.

She'd been living in the tiny flat that the craft shop rented out. Accessed via the close at the side of the shop, and then through to an excuse for a garden. Stone steps, where the greenery of potted plants clung on to the metal railings, led to her front door.

Nothing looked straight. Everything from the curve of the steps to the arched close, twisted and wound its way to wherever it was supposed to go.

And Mari was fine with that. It reminded her of her life. She'd taken a bit of an excursion recently from living in one of the quaint coastal towns north of Edinburgh where she'd commuted over the bridge to the city to the accountancy firm, and now lived in the heart of the pretty city. An unexpected small windfall, a handy inheritance from an aunt she barely knew, had allowed her to make the longed–for leap to being self–employed.

In practical terms, she made money from her knitting. Selling items from her website and from the craft shop. She'd started teaching knitting classes at the craft shop too, once a fortnight. Now, by popular demand, once a week. It didn't pay a lot of money, but it was enough to prevent her dipping into her small savings. And that was fine for now. The ability to manage past clients' accounts gave her the experience to handle her own finances, frugally, or sensibly as she preferred to think of it.

But the knitting wasn't her true vocation. Not the one she secretly pinned her hopes and dreams on. Like most dreams, it had remained elusive. However, she'd reached a point in her life when it was sort of now or never.

Wrestling with the door key, jiggling it around until it clicked open, she stepped inside her little bolthole.

Autumn sunlight fought its way through the living room window, cast a glow into the single bedroom across the colourful rugs, and ran out of steam by the time it reached the compact kitchen. Mari flicked the light on.

She'd barely set her groceries down on the kitchen table, when a message came through on her phone from Ivy, the owner of the craft shop:

Do you have the Fair Isle style jumper finished? A customer has ordered it.

Yes, I'll bring it down.

Grabbing the jumper, along with the hat and scarf she'd knitted, Mari hurried down the stairs, through the close and into the craft shop. The windows looked out on to the busy cobbled street where tourists and local residents went by, many pausing to peer into the pretty shop.

Ivy, fifty and fit, had blond hair shot through with glitter strands, and smiled at Mari.

'The orders have been coming in for more knitwear now that the summer's gone. People are thinking about their cosy winter clothes. I'd like to get them posted off today.'

Mari gave Ivy the colourful jumper. 'And I finished the hat and scarf last night too.' She handed over the extras.

Evenings spent knitting in the cosy flat were relaxing while being productive. The accommodation was indeed basic, with a living room, bedroom, kitchen and bathroom. The rooms weren't big enough to swing a squirrel never mind a cat. But the view...the view was magnificent.

In the evenings, the city glittered as if encrusted with fairy diamonds. The architecture was silhouetted against the night skies that Mari loved to gaze at.

And she loved the history of the building. She was living in the present in a property that had changed very little and retained a sense of the past. Crafts had added to the cosy homeliness of the flat, with one of Ivy's patchwork quilts on the bed, appliqué cushions, ditsy print curtains, a crocheted blanket on the couch, quilted oven mitts, egg cosies and a tea cosy. Ivy's handiwork was lovely.

Mari had been fortunate to snap up the lease when she'd seen it advertised via the craft shop. As well as selling some of her knitwear in the shop, she helped Ivy with her accounts. It was a win–win for both of them.

Having moved to the city halfway through the summertime, Mari felt she was living her own Midsummer Night's Dream. Now the chance to submit her new play to the theatre dangled enticingly in her thoughts.

Ivy was delighted with the knitted items, and they had already established a fair share for the garments Mari knitted. Skilled in knitting intricate patterns to a high standard, and working fast, Mari was a valued member of the close–knit crafters supplying Ivy's shop.

The shop itself was a distraction for Mari. Shelves were stocked with a lovely range of yarn. Rolls of fabric from quilting weight cotton to dressmaking satin, lined part of the shop. There were threads on carousels, embroidery thread to crewel wool. Patterns and kits were popular with customers, along with haberdashery items.

As Ivy carefully folded the jumper to parcel it up for posting, Mari took a moment to chat to her.

'Do you know anything about the theatre further up the street?' said Mari. 'I've walked past it numerous times and never even knew it was there.'

'Oh, it's easy to walk by without noticing it. I've never been to any of their shows. I'm not into the theatre. I like to go to the cinema or watch the telly. But I read about the two businessmen that bought the theatre to restore it back to its former glory. They're both rich from their wealthy backgrounds and from working in the stock market, and poured their own money into it. That would be a couple of years ago. It's open now. They had shows on during the summer.'

'Do the businessmen run the theatre, or do they have a manager for that?'

'They both run it themselves. They have staff to help. But they're young men, in their early thirties.' Ivy smiled. 'And handsome. I've heard that one of them in particular, Huntly. He's a heartbreaker.'

'You've never met them,' said Mari.

'No, but I've heard the gossip. The other man, Niall, is a looker too. They're both single. They date models and actresses. The gossip is they split up with their latest girlfriends earlier this year. Niall's model girlfriend left to live in New York, and Huntly had a fireworks ending with the actress he was dating outside the theatre.'

'That sounds so dramatic,' Mari remarked.

Ivy shrugged. 'That's what I heard. But now they're focused on getting the theatre up and running successfully. I know you love going to the theatre. You should check their website to see what's on.'

'I'll do that,' Mari confirmed, planning to scour it for any information. 'Okay, see you later. I'll pop down around two this afternoon to teach the knitting class.'

'Great. It's fully booked. If you continue to draw people in, I'll have to buy more folding chairs to seat them in the shop.' Ivy's comment was half-joking, half earnest.

Smiling, Mari headed out, but felt she was being watched.

Looking across at the shop that was always closed, yet seemed to still be in business, she saw the black cat watching her.

Spindle apparently belonged to the elusive owner, a man who sold curiosities and second-hand specialities, whatever those were. Mari hadn't an inkling. According to whoever she spoke to, the owner was a tall, thin man, or portly, well-dressed in a three-piece suit complete with a pocket watch, or casual bordering on scruffy. She'd decided it didn't matter as she'd never seen him. Only his cat. And Spindle had a curious habit of—

She glanced up the street, thinking for a second about the theatre, and when she looked back, the cat had gone.

Shrugging off any thoughts about the cat, she went upstairs to her flat and made herself tea and buttered toast for breakfast. Eating at the comfy seat near the living room window that provided the view she so loved, she mulled over whether to submit her play to the theatre.

She'd had a spark of an idea for a while, brewing in her imagination when she lived in the small coastal town. When she'd moved to Edinburgh, the curious shop opposite had made the sparks ignite into the missing parts of the story, a three–act play, featuring a strange and magical shop, tucked into a cobbled street in a historic part of the city. A shop that sold everything. And a watchful cat with an uncanny knack of disappearing. A fictional story, based mainly on Mari's imagination with a little intriguing embellishment.

Taking a deep breath, Mari pressed the send button, having decided to take a chance and submit her play to the theatre before heading down to teach the knitting class.

As she sat amid the ladies seated at two long tables, helping them practice everything from how to cast on stitches to knitting in the round, she wondered if anyone at the theatre had opened the attachment and seen her play yet.

The most likely response she told herself was a silent no. Followed by a thanks but no thanks. And she didn't want to dwell on a reply tearing into her work, though she knew that came with the territory. She'd checked out the theatre's website that revealed little more than Ivy had told her. They needed to supply more information about their forthcoming shows, pictures from past shows, though they did have a handful.

But there was nothing of note about Huntly or Niall, or any pictures showing how handsome they were. If that was true. But she was inclined to believe Ivy as the craft shop was a hive of gossip as well as creativity.

'The ladies were hoping you'd demonstrate how you spin your own yarn using a drop spindle,' Ivy reminded Mari.

'Oh, yes.' Mari dug into her knitting bag and pulled out the small wooden drop spindle and a bag filled with soft wool fibres ready for spinning into a strand of yarn.

Fascinated faces circled round as Mari showed them how easy it was to spin their own yarn. 'You have to practice, to get the feel of it, how to gently tease the wool fibres out so that they spin around the spindle.'

Ivy had ordered in a box of spindles. They were small and inexpensive, intending to let them try using them.

Laughter and smiles filled the craft shop that afternoon as the class members all had a go at spinning yarn. Everyone left with a spindle with their first hand spun piece of yarn around it. Ivy sold the lot. No one wanted to give them back again.

Mari promised to give them another spinning lesson soon. The members promised to practice their new skill in time to then learn how to ply the yarn.

'That went well,' Ivy said to Mari as they tidied away the folding tables and chairs.

'It did. I'm glad they enjoyed it.'

'You have a knack for teaching knitting. A lot of patience and knowledge to pass on. I think you'll find you made the right decision to leave your accountancy job to have a go at making a living from knitting and crafts.'

And writing plays, Mari thought, wondering if she'd had a response to her submission. Even an acknowledgement that they'd received it.

Surreptitiously checking her phone for messages, she sighed. Nothing yet.

'Everything okay, Mari?' said Ivy.

'Yes,' she fibbed.

As customers came into the craft shop, Mari cleared the last of her knitting away, and headed up to her flat.

Filling the kettle for a cup of late afternoon tea before starting to think what she'd make for dinner, she jumped when a message came through on her phone.

And there it was, a reply from Niall at the theatre.

Dear Marigold, it began.

Mari muttered to herself, forgetting that her full name had been on the front page of the play, even though she'd submitted it under Mari. Anyway...

We'd like to discuss your play with you, and would be obliged if you could come to the theatre today. Short notice, but I see you're living a stone's throw from the theatre. If you could pop in, we'd like to chat to you.

Mari's heart thundered like she hadn't felt in a long time. Not since splitting up with her last boyfriend when he'd ditched her horribly for the new love of his life. That had been over a year now, but the feeling resurfaced. She immediately suppressed it and took a steadying breath.

Grab your bag and go, she urged herself. Forget the tea. Forget everything. Just go.

And so she did.

The relatively short walk up the cobbled street seemed to take ages, and if she hadn't thought she'd attract unwanted attention, she'd have sprinted there. She could run in these boots. She'd worn the clothes from the morning. They looked tidy, and matched the city, unintentionally.

Her hair hung in soft, silky waves around her shoulders. And she'd refreshed her rose lipstick while locking her front door with the iffy key.

Seeing the theatre now ahead, she tried to calm herself down. They'd sense her nervousness, and it would surely do her no favours in the interview. Or chat. Or whatever they intended.

Come on, she bolstered herself. Don't waste this chance. And the challenging part of her nature kicked in, like it had done on days when she could've cheerfully walked out of the accountancy firm when the pressure was crushing her. But she'd tholed it. Now, she could do this. There had to be something about her play that had piqued their interest. Busy men like them wouldn't burn their time if they thought it was nonsense.

This thought gave her the steely confidence to walk into the shadowed theatre, leaving the remnants of the fading golden sunlight behind her on the cobbled street.

The atmosphere was a mix of theatres she'd been in. A small foyer and box office where tickets were sold, bookings made, unmanned. The burgundy and gold colour scheme created a rich, traditional decor, with velvet and brocade fabrics adding to the styling. She felt her boots sink into the plush carpeting.

'Hello,' she called tentatively through to the office behind the front desk, hoping that someone was there to show her through to meet Niall.

Silence from the foyer area, but then she heard angry voices drifting from the auditorium. Arrows indicated the direction for theatre goers to take, so she followed them, hearing the voices, one man in particular, shouting.

'On guard!'

And then a clash of swords.

CHAPTER TWO

Mari stood at the back of the empty auditorium watching a scene from a play being rehearsed on stage. A man, tall and fit, was wearing white fencing gear — white jacket, breeches, gloves and a protective mask that shielded his face. He wielded a foil sword and was play fighting two actors portraying medieval costumed dragons.

The man seemed proficient in fencing and appeared to be instructing the two actors, and several others dressed as villagers, on how to perform an action–packed scene. Mari assumed it was for a forthcoming stage play at the theatre.

Whipping his sword, he lunged across the stage, showing them how to perform the moves with energy and aplomb.

She pictured an audience would be engrossed in such a performance, and the theatre filled with excitement.

The interior of the theatre was larger than she'd anticipated. From the outside, she imagined it would be quite small, an intimate experience. But the auditorium's capacity was probably well over three hundred, and then she saw that there was a balcony adding a substantial number of seats.

The structure seemed to stretch deeper into a niche in the cobbled street, extending to accommodate all the comfy seats and a fairly large stage.

Anyone sitting in the stalls, near the front of the stage, would have a thrilling time seeing the action up close. But the way the auditorium was designed, Mari felt that everyone from those sitting in the middle stalls and further back, to those in the slightly raised dress circle, and in the box seats at the sides of the stage, wouldn't miss a moment of the performance.

The stage lighting, even for a rehearsal, created a forest setting with a sense of depth and highlighted the main characters against a backdrop of tree–painted scenery.

She was impressed by the theatre, liking the atmosphere of it. Impressed too, by the elusive fencer, wondering if perchance he was Niall.

Another tall man, early thirties, wearing expensive casuals, stood down at the front of the stage, holding a copy of the play, following along with the action, but making no comment. As if sensing he was being watched, he glanced round, and when he saw Mari standing there, he immediately came walking up the centre aisle to greet her. He had well–styled blond hair and an easy smile.

'I'm looking for Niall,' said Mari. 'To discuss my play.'

'Thanks for popping along at such short notice. I'm Niall.' His eyes were a lovely pale grey with dark lashes, and he was certainly a looker.

But she wasn't here to admire Niall, or anyone else. She wanted to discuss her play.

A clash of swords sounded again from the stage as the fighting continued.

'We're rehearsing an action scene,' Niall explained, glancing back at the activity on the stage.

'Is this for a forthcoming play at the theatre?' She would've been interested to see it.

'No, a drama group needed a proper stage to rehearse their show, and we offered to let them use ours this afternoon,' Niall explained.

'It looks exciting.' The type of show she'd enjoy seeing. 'Dragons and drama.'

Niall cast her a warm smile. 'We're currently planning our new schedule for the late autumn and winter. We'd scheduled a play for the autumn, but then we found out that it had been performed twice before, and we're looking for completely original plays that have never been seen by audiences. That's why we're keen to find new material lickety–split.'

'You mentioned in your message that you wanted to discuss my play,' she prompted him, eager to know what he thought.

'We read the first act, and were impressed by the quality of the writing and loved the elements of secrets and a little touch of magic from the shop owner and his cat. Huntly is particularly keen on the atmosphere of this mysterious shop that sells everything, and loved that it's set in the past rather than the present.'

'I thought it suited the theme,' said Mari.

'It does, and we have a wonderful selection of costumes that we could use, and actors we think would suit the leading roles. We'd done a lot of prep work for the show we had to cancel, and there's plenty we can reuse and adapt.'

Mari's hopes soared.

'We're thinking of a traditional type setting,' Niall elaborated. 'That whole atmosphere with a wintry feeling, dark nights by the fire, lanterns and cobblestones.'

The way he described it made Mari's heart beat with excitement. 'So you're interested in my play.'

'We are. I'm not sure how much you know about our theatre.'

'Very little. I only came across it this morning, and saw the notice in the window.'

'Huntly wrote the notice quickly as we'd decided we needed to hurry up and find another play.'

'The writing was stylish.'

'Everything Huntly does is stylish,' he said with a friendly smile. 'We've known each other since university. We were both studying the arts, drama, music, literature. And Huntly belonged to a fencing club. He's the sporting type. Adept at everything he does.' Niall glanced at his friend still slaying dragons on the stage.

'Do either of you act in the plays?' she said.

'No, we're not actors. Though I'm sure that Huntly would succeed if he ever decided to step into the thespian spotlight.' The grey eyes looked at her. 'Do you act?'

'No, not at all.' Except when she was pretending to be calm and confident when her stomach was filled with butterflies.

Niall paused, seeing the rehearsal draw to a close. He waved eagerly to the fencer. 'Huntly! Marigold is here.'

'Mari,' she said lightly.

Niall took this in and nodded, but he gestured to Huntly again.

Discarding his gloves, Huntly unfastened the front of his white jacket. It flapped open, exposing his leanly muscled bare chest as he strode towards them, keeping a grip on the prop sword. A loop attached to the handle of the foil was around his wrist to prevent him from dropping it.

Mari couldn't see his face because he was still wearing the mask.

As he got closer, he pulled the mask off.

If Huntly had wanted to make a dramatic first impression on Mari, he'd achieved it, with bells on. The handsome but unsmiling face, as pale as Niall's, indeed belonged to a heartbreaker. Blue eyes, the colour of sapphires, appraised the pretty young woman standing beside Niall and probably came up short. At least, that was Mari's assessment. Unlike her first impression of him, tall, handsome, fit, with thick dark hair tumbling in unruly curls over his forehead. The type of hair she felt the urge to run her fingers through and get up to all sorts of mischief.

Both men were well over six feet tall and towered above her, but Mari stood her ground, bolstered by the comments Niall had made about her play.

'This is Marigold. Mari.' Niall quickly corrected himself, introducing her to Huntly.

The sapphire eyes looked down at her, and he frowned.

'The playwright,' Niall reminded him.

Mari baulked at being called a playwright. It was flattering, but she felt it was misleading as she'd yet to have any play accepted.

Before she could clarify this, Huntly's rich, deep, voice resonated in the theatre. 'Has your play ever been performed before?' This, more than anything, would decide whether the conversation ended right there or not.

'No, I've never had any of my plays performed.'

This was news to Huntly and Niall.

Huntly glanced at him for an explanation. Niall didn't have one.

'We assumed from the quality of your writing, the structure of the acts, the dialogue and stage notes that you were experienced,' said Niall, without accusation or disappointment.

'The notice in the window didn't state that as a requirement,' Mari said in her defence.

This was true.

'If I'd known, I wouldn't have submitted my play,' she added.

The glance Niall exchanged with Huntly was clear. It was their own fault.

'Can you tell me a bit about your background,' said Huntly.

'I worked for two accountancy firms, several years at each, and recently gave up my job to take a chance on being self–employed, selling my knitting—'

'I was referring to your background in *writing plays*,' Huntly cut–in.

Mari squirmed and a blush started to form across her cheeks. 'I've written a few plays, and *The Shop That Sells Everything* is my latest. I wrote it during the summer when I moved to the city from the small town I belong to further up the east coast.'

'To take a chance on finding success as a playwright,' Huntly summarised.

Mari nodded. 'I inherited a small amount of money, and decided to use it to help support myself while I wrote my plays. I'd intended writing while working in accounts, but...' She shook her head. 'The two didn't mix well. It was hard to be creative after doing accountancy work all day. And often I had to work weekends, or attend financial business conferences.'

'And the knitting?' Huntly prompted her further.

'I rent a tiny flat above the craft shop near here. I sell my knitting, jumpers, cardigans, various garments, and teach knitting classes in the shop too. It helps to keep my savings intact.'

She gestured to the jumper and cardigan jacket she was wearing as an example of her knitting skills.

'They look shop bought,' said Niall, impressed.

'I'll take that as a compliment,' she said.

Huntly looked thoughtful and summed up Mari's skills. 'So you're a knitter with aspirations to be a playwright.'

She wasn't sure if he intended to sound so blunt, or knock the wind out of her sails. His assessment of her was accurate, and yet...it turned her inside out.

Huntly wasn't finished. 'We're certainly looking for a diamond of a play in the rough. But it has to be a sparkling gem. We won't have time to polish it.'

A wave of tense emotion washed over her, and she felt the urge to run.

'I'm sorry, I think I've made a mistake,' she muttered. And then she headed out, walking briskly from the auditorium, following the arrows in the opposite direction to the foyer, past the front desk and pushed the doors open, feeling the need to escape from the theatre and the embarrassing situation she'd put herself in.

Inside, Niall glared at Huntly. 'That was harsh.'

Huntly sighed heavily and agreed. Huffing at his own bluntness, he strode after her, out into the fading sunlight.

Proving that she could run in her boots, Mari was well ahead of him, not imagining either of them would chase after her. But rather the urge to flee taking hold of her common sense. Scarpering out the theatre and bolting down the cobbled street was the type of thing to attract attention, which was the last thing she wanted.

'Marigold, wait!' Huntly called after her.

She kept going. No glancing back. She recognised the haughty voice that had stung her to the core.

'Marigold!' he repeated, with no success.

Ignoring people's startled reactions to him wearing his fencing whites, jacket flapping open revealing his chest, and carrying the prop sword that he didn't have time to untie from his wrist, Huntly ran after her, closing the gap.

'Mari!' he shouted.

At the sound of her name, she jolted, paused and glanced round at the tall, determined man hurrying towards her.

'Come back,' he said, his deep voice filtering into the glow of the early evening.

Without a word, she shook her head. Her feelings were cast to the wind. She wasn't the type to burst into tears, but for some reason, she was close to it. Mixed emotions bubbled up inside her.

Huntly stopped running. He stood there looking at her, his sword dangling forlornly at his side. 'I'm sorry I was grumpy, Mari. But I've been slaying dragons all afternoon.'

Mari blinked. That was his excuse?

For some reason, this made her smile, and she gazed over at him as they stood there in a standoff.

She shook her head at him in dismay. 'That's the most ridiculous excuse, but actually true, that I've ever heard.'

Huntly looked hopeful. 'Come back, so we can talk about your play.'

She wasn't prepared to relent easily. Neither was she prepared for the tourists and others taking an inordinate interest in them, snapping pictures of them, particularly of Huntly.

'You're creating a scene,' she scolded him. 'People are looking at you with that outfit and the sword.'

'It's a prop,' he argued, showing how it dangled from his wrist.

'They don't know that. It looks real. You're causing a furore.' And she was in the heart of it.

Huntly was about to argue again, but then he saw the number of people taking pictures of them.

'Run,' he urged her.

Mari hesitated.

Grabbing her hand, Huntly started to run towards the theatre to get away from the crowd's interest, taking Mari with him.

'Nooo,' she shouted, feeling his strength pull her along at speed. Racing to keep up with him, they ran together towards the entrance of the theatre, but another part of the crowd of onlookers had closed in, blocking their way.

Huntly pivoted, whirling Mari around in another direction.

'Run, Mari! Run!' he urged her.

'Where are we going?' she shouted at him.

'The old entrance to the theatre.'

A wrought iron gate was ahead of them at the side of the theatre, under an archway. They ran towards it.

It was only when they reached the gate that she realised something was missing. 'There's no key.' Then she added. 'There's no lock either!'

Ignoring her last comment, Huntly let the sword dangle from his wrist, and stuck his hands through a gap between the iron bars of the gate that looked like it belonged to a bygone era.

She watched him twist and turn his hands and wrists around, virtually in thin air, or so it looked to her, and then the gate clicked open.

'In you go,' he said, sweeping her through, following close behind, and then shut the gate firmly. It locked again with a loud click.

'No one can follow us now,' he assured her. But he was concerned that people could snap pictures of them through the gate.

They continued hurrying along a narrow pathway.

'How did you do that?' she said. 'There was no key, no lock.'

'So you think.'

'What does that mean?'

'There's a knack to it. I'll show you another time so you can use it if you're ever in this situation again.'

'That's hardly likely,' she scoffed.

'I have a tendency to attract drama.'

'Appropriate for your line of work,' she quipped.

He glanced at her. 'Be flippant all you want, but fair warning, if you become involved with me, the drama on stage may not be all you experience.'

The assuredness of his warning made her rethink his offer to teach her how to open the gate that had no key or lock.

By now they were running down a few stone steps, then immediately heading up another set, until they reached a level that Mari wasn't sure was up or down.

'Where are we?' she called to him as he bounded ahead.

'Almost there.'

'Where?'

'Here.' He opened a door that led into the back of the theatre.

Before following him inside, she glanced at the depth of the building that confirmed how deep the structure was. And high. Craning to look up, she saw that the front part rose up three levels. The top resembled a castle turret.

'I live up there,' Huntly told her.

'In the turret?'

'It's a sort of castellated structure. I stay overnight when I've been working late at the theatre. I have a house in another area of Edinburgh, but this is a handy bolthole with a wonderful view of the city, especially in the evenings.'

'I live in one of those above the craft shop. Not a turret, but a cosy bolthole with a great view.'

'Something else we have in common,' he said.

She wondered what else they shared.

'Apart from a love of the theatre,' he added.

'I do love going to see plays in the city. There's so much here to entertain. I used to travel from the town I lived in to enjoy nights out at the theatres in Edinburgh.' She told him the name of the town.

'I've never been to the town, but a friend of mine lives there. Wil opened a dance studio in the town recently. Perhaps you're acquainted with him. Wil's quite a well–known dancer.'

'I heard about the new dance studio, and I'm familiar with Wil's name. He's a wonderful dancer. I saw him perform last year in Edinburgh. But I'd left the town before his studio was up and running.'

'You'll have a chance to meet him, if you become involved with the theatre. I'm letting him use the stage for his new dance show rehearsals.'

'Will the dance show be part of the theatre's autumn or winter line–up?'

'We're not sure yet. The schedules have to be decided, and Wil's still designing the new choreography. He's able to practice in his studio, but needs to see how the show would work on stage.'

'How many plays are you planning to schedule for the theatre for the coming seasons?' she said.

'A few, including yours, if we can chat and come to some agreement about how to make it work. I didn't mean to sound snippy when I said there won't be time to polish your play.'

'I understand if it's for such a tight schedule.'

'But I think it won't need a lot of polishing. If the second and third acts are as engaging as the first, then it'll be fine.'

Her heart picked up hope. She thought that those acts were stronger than the opening.

He took a deep breath. 'There's a feeling to nights like this that I'd like us to try and capture in your play. The mysterious shop sounds intriguing, and I was impressed with your notes on stage settings. I can picture how we'd create the shop so that audiences would be fascinated with it.'

And in that moment, Mari sensed that Huntly had read the opening act of her play and understood what she was trying to portray.

'I apologise again, Mari, for being grumpy.' His handsome face was highlighted in the evening's amber glow as he looked at her.

'It's fine,' she said. 'You'd been slaying dragons all afternoon.'

He smiled at her, causing her heart to react.

Before they went inside the theatre, Mari glanced around at the early evening glow in the sky arching above them. She breathed in the scent of the mild autumn air. And the sense of excitement she often felt living in the city. Though tonight, there was an extra edge of excitement, being here with Huntly the heartbreaker and a magnet for drama.

Dipping his head slightly under the lintel of the door, he led them into the theatre.

A light glowed along the far end of a corridor. Huntly flicked other lights on to illuminate various nooks and crannies that darted off in different directions.

Huntly gestured to the areas as they walked along. 'The dressing rooms for the actors are over there. And across from them is wardrobe.'

The dressing rooms were in darkness, but Mari pictured the dressing table mirrors edged with lights, and an array of makeup and pent up tension before a performance.

Rows and rows of rails were filled with all sorts of costumes hanging neatly, and organised into sections, rather like a department store's clothing. Red jackets trimmed with gold braid hung alongside tailcoats and a classic mackintosh that she imagined a detective character might wear. A thick wool trench coat was beside a long, black wool cape teamed with a top hat.

Trousers, breeches, jeans and pantaloons were next.

But it was the dresses that made her pause. A classic tea dress with a rose print caught her eye, and a beaded little twenties flapper dress. Then there was the glamorous glint from a gold Art Deco number, but it was the fairytale ballgown that she gazed at. Layers of pale blue chiffon sparkled under the lighting as if sprinkled with stars. It was sequins and beads sew on, but what a dress to make an entrance with on stage.

Huntly glanced back at her.

'Sorry, I was admiring the dresses,' she said, hurrying along to catch up with him.

'We were fortunate to inherit a lot of the costumes from the original stock in the theatre when we took it over,' he explained. 'And we've scoured continually for any costumes we can get our hands on. Some bought in job lots. So we're quite well–stocked. And I'm planning to buy more that I've been offered. A real bargain, and there are probably a few that would suit your play.'

Feelings of excitement charged through her. 'I'd love to take a peek.'

'I'll show you the email when we get to the office. It included plenty of pictures. We hire wardrobe staff and they're skilled in altering the costumes too. We don't have an expert knitter like you though,' he said, casting a smile back at her.

Mari smiled, and then tried to keep up. His long legs strode along the corridor with ease, but she had to put a spurt on so she wasn't left behind.

His sword clattered off the wall as he gestured to another area. 'Props are kept over there, and we have extra stored upstairs.' Taming his sword, he continued. 'Scenery is backstage and we have a wonderful set director in charge of that and the lighting.'

The route they'd taken led past the rear of the stage where she saw scenery backgrounds stacked up, some like a pack of cards, layers of different types of greenery, painted shop fronts, a fake street scene and a seascape with little yachts and a cloudless blue sky.

Huntly paused at a large section of a night cityscape. 'I call this our starry night sky. It could work well for your play, creating the dark, cosy evening atmosphere I pictured when I read the opening scenes in the first act.'

Mari's eyes scanned the inky blue skyline. It looked almost black at the top and faded to lighter midnight tones towards the bottom where the outlines of the city's spires and buildings were beautiful silhouettes. Stars painted in dazzling white and golden yellow gave the impression that they were sparkling in the night sky.

'Is this Edinburgh at night?' she said.

'An artistic impression of it. I think it's better to have a feeling of the skyline rather than an exact replica.'

Mari agreed. 'The shop and the city I've featured in my play is like that. It's not real, just what my imagination portrays.'

'Is the shop somewhere you've been? Or seen? It felt like you knew it well.'

'There's a shop across from the craft shop. I can see it from the window of my flat upstairs. It sells curiosities and second–hand treasures, whatever they are.'

'You've not been inside it?'

'No, it's always closed. Though nowadays people can run their businesses online, from their websites, like I do. So it doesn't mean that the shop is abandoned. It certainly doesn't look any different from the way it was when I first saw it. It's been kept clean and tidy, so someone must be tending to it in the midnight hours when we're all fast asleep. Or whenever.'

'An interesting shop by the sounds of it. I must pop down and have a look.'

'My play really is only based on the feeling of it, not the actual shop,' she insisted.

He nodded. 'I understand. And it's the atmosphere we want to create for the audience to become engrossed in the fantastical story. Your shop has elements of mystery and a touch of magic. Where else would a shop that sold everything exist. Where customers can go in and ask for anything from an ancient map to a specific Victorian teapot, and the exact first edition of a vintage book.'

She was impressed. Huntly had obviously read the opening of her play.

'Or a modern item, like an electric guitar or a baby grand piano,' he said.

'I can easily adapt the instruments to suit your props. I noticed a violin back there among the props. That would be fine instead of a piano.'

Huntly frowned at her. 'Didn't you notice our piano sitting at the side of the stage? It was there when I was fighting the dragons.'

'No, I didn't. I was too busy watching you.' The comment was out before she could stifle it, making it sound as if she'd been so enamoured with Huntly that something as large as the piano had escaped her notice. But it was true. She had admired Huntly and clearly missed the piano.

She blushed and wished they could move on because she felt in the spotlight of the overhead lamp.

Huntly smiled. 'And I'll take that as a compliment.'

'I didn't mean—' She went to object but he started to walk on.

'The cat intrigues me, but we obviously can't have a real cat in the play,' he said, heading through to the auditorium and walking up the centre aisle and through to where the corridor lead to the foyer.

'No, I thought a stuffed toy black cat would suffice.'

Huntly grinned at her. Such a sexy smile as he walked through to the office behind the front desk. 'Perhaps I'll find one in that curious shop when I pop down to have a nosy at it.'

'Find what in what shop?' Niall said as they walked in. He was sitting at the office desk that had a chair on either side, and appeared to be reading Mari's play.

Earlier, he'd been working on their accounts. The computer screen showed a spreadsheet of figures, just a mass of numbers to most people, but to a maths magpie like Mari, she read it like a book. And reacted, then tried to hide her reaction from them. But Huntly noticed. Niall was none the wiser.

'A stuffed fake cat in a curious shop further down the street,' Huntly summarised.

Niall didn't balk. 'Okay.'

Huntly changed the subject. 'Mari has decided to forgive me for being a prat.'

'Thank goodness, because you caused such a commotion running amok with your silly sword,' Niall

31

told him. 'People came scurrying in, warning me and wanting to know if I knew what was going on.'

'What did you tell them?' said Huntly.

'I crossed my fingers, leaned at an angle, and told a little white fib, a slanted version of the truth.' Niall made the gestures as he explained. 'I told them it was part of the theatre's promotion for a new and exciting play we're planning for the autumn. Everyone left happy. A few gave me their names for us to tell them when the opening night is so they can buy tickets.'

'Wonderful.' Huntly went over to a table in the corner where tea things were set up and flicked the kettle on. Then he glanced round at Mari, and joked. 'This means you'll have to give us your play so that Niall isn't caught out on telling porky pies.'

'There isn't a man dressed in white fencing gear wielding a sword in the play,' Mari told them playfully.

Huntly brushed such a triviality aside and finally untied the sword from his wrist. 'It's the shop that sells everything. Even annoying men like me.'

Mari laughed, but her eyes kept glancing at the accounts on the computer screen.

They both noticed her looking this time.

'Sorry, I don't mean to pry.' She raised her hand to shield the screen to show that she wasn't deliberately poking her nose into their business.

Huntly sighed heavily. 'Okay, is there something wrong with our accounts?'

'I'm one of those people that can look at a load of numbers and see if they add up or not,' she explained.

But she didn't want to tell them in case she was wrong.

'Spit it out,' Huntly urged her.

Mari took a deep breath. 'I think you've got a leaky ship.'

Huntly and Niall frowned.

'You're losing money, inadvertently, and it's leaking out of your main revenue figures. There's a mistake in your calculations, and I think you've been carrying it forward month by month. I've seen errors like this a few times with clients.'

'Could you throw us a lifeline to save the ship going down?' said Huntly.

'It's an easy adjustment,' she said confidently. 'What I call a tea break task.'

Huntly brightened as the kettle clicked off. 'Tea coming right up.'

Niall gestured to the chair he'd been sitting in getting their accounts wrong. 'It's all yours, Mari.'

While they drank their tea, she tackled the accounts. It was an easy task for someone with her experience.

'There you go. Sorted.' She leaned back and let them see the screen.

They got up from their chairs and came round to look at the figures.

'That was fast,' Niall muttered. 'I've barely dunked my biscuit.'

'We're definitely keeping Mari,' Huntly said to Niall.

'Oh, yes,' Niall agreed.

'So, let's talk money,' Huntly said to Mari, sitting down again at the desk, while Niall pulled up his chair to join them.

Huntly's bluntness jolted her.

'We'll obviously have to read the other two acts of your play before we make a firm offer,' Huntly added.

Mari nodded. 'I understand.'

'But provided they're as well–written and entertaining as your opening act, I think we've got our next production on our hands,' said Huntly.

'While you two were running around outside, I've been reading through the second act and it's even more exciting,' said Niall.

Mari took a sip of her tea to wash down the urge to cheer with glee.

CHAPTER THREE

After her meeting with Huntly and Niall, Mari left the theatre and walked home down the cobbled street. She breathed in the heady scent of the autumn air. It was one of those lovely mild evenings, and the cafes and eateries were busy with people enjoying themselves. The windows were aglow with lights and activity, but she longed for the cosy calm of her flat, to unwind after the whirlwind of the day.

Music and chatter from the lively social life buzzed in the back of her thoughts as she replayed Huntly's blunt parting remark.

'We'll read the complete play and contact you tomorrow,' said Huntly, and then added, 'And it's our policy now not to become romantically involved with anyone we work with. It complicates everything.'

Huntly's bluntness was going to be an acquired taste, but this policy suited her. There would be no misinterpreting friendly banter for flirting, or any romantic involvements being jeopardised when the inevitable clashes of artistic differences emerged.

Mari had smiled, nodded, and then left.

The aroma from the cafes and eateries reminded her that she'd missed dinner. Butterflies of excitement had filled her stomach, but now she felt ready to have something to eat. She planned to make an easy dinner when she got home.

The craft shop was closed for the night, but as she approached, she saw the lights were on inside. Ivy's husband was helping her restock the shelves with bolts of fabric. She couldn't hear their laughter, but she could see it through the window of the craft shop. Mari hoped one day to have a happy marriage like that.

Ivy's husband, Bob, worked as a baker, so there was no shortage of doughnuts, yum yums and cupcakes at the knitting classes. Ivy told Mari that her biggest success was accepting his proposal. They'd married young, and were clearly still happy together.

They were so engrossed in each other that they didn't notice Mari walk past.

Mari headed through the close and up to her flat.

Flicking a lamp on to cast a warm glow in the living room, she went through to the kitchen, and after rummaging around, decided to make herself a tasty snack of cheese on toast and a mug of tea.

Carrying it through to the living room, she sat in the comfy chair near the window, gazing out at her favourite view. This evening, it reminded her of the starry night backdrop Huntly had shown her. To think that her play might come to life at the theatre was amazing. But she'd had her dreams crushed too many times before, so until they'd contacted her in the morning and said whether they wanted her play or not, she decided to fill the remainder of her evening with the one thing guaranteed to help her unwind — knitting.

'Mari's nice, isn't she?' Niall said to Huntly, shrugging his jacket on and getting ready to leave the theatre for the night.

Huntly eased the tension from his shoulders. He'd changed out of his fencing whites into a white shirt, waistcoat and dark trousers. They'd both been sitting in the office reading through Mari's play and discussing how they'd produce it. 'She is.'

'Don't break her heart,' Niall told him.

Huntly scoffed at the remark. 'I've no intention of breaking anyone's heart.' Then he threw the comment back at Niall. 'Don't you mess with her heart either.'

'I won't. You're the one with a reputation as a heartbreaker,' Niall reminded him.

Huntly didn't need to be reminded. He still bore the scorch marks from his last fiery break–up with his ex–girlfriend.

'Remember, Scarlet is bound to hear about the new play and want a lead role.'

This was another reminder Huntly didn't need. He'd never dated Scarlet and had no romantic interest in her, but she'd tried several times to become his new girlfriend, without success.

'There's no role to suit her,' said Huntly. 'Besides, she's a disruptive element, and we don't want that for the rest of the cast or others involved in the production.'

Satisfied that he'd warned his friend of any forthcoming furore, Niall left. 'See you in the morning.'

'Goodnight.'

Sighing wearily, the thought of driving home didn't appeal to Huntly, so he turned the lights off, secured the theatre, peeled his handwritten notice off the window, and then headed upstairs to his turret to cook dinner.

An excellent cook, he considered what to make in his beautifully kitted out kitchen. Chef level saucepans and other professional accoutrements hung on the walls. Lifting up a skillet, he whipped up the ingredients to make a soufflé omelette, and then cooked it on the stove, adding a sprinkling of grated cheese and herbs.

Serving it up with a crisp green salad, he sat down to dinner for one at the kitchen table. Every room in the turret offered a panoramic view of Edinburgh at night, sparkling all around him. The views stretched across the cityscape, and he found his thoughts drifting to Mari, wondering if she was enjoying the views from her bolthole.

Mari always had a few knitting projects on the go, and picked up the rich, cream Aran knit jumper she'd been working on. One sleeve to knit and it would be finished. Another garment she'd sell in the craft shop. She'd had her own cotton fabric labels printed with her name and a flower logo, and stitched these into everything she knitted.

All her garments were well finished, and she put the Aran jumper pieces aside ready to be stitched together. She had similar jumpers in stock in her flat. The classic colours were always popular.

Checking her website, she noticed several orders for the knitted hats and scarves she'd listed for sale, and packed these up ready for posting in the morning, before continuing to finish the sleeve.

Gazing out at the view, she wondered if Huntly had gone home to his house, or if he was up in his turret admiring his own view of the city.

Clearing away the dishes and tidying up his kitchen, Huntly couldn't shake off the feeling of restlessness. He wasn't sure what had gotten into him. Usually, after a busy day, he'd unwind and sleep like a log until the dawn. But tonight...

Looking out at the calm night, he decided to head out and take an evening stroll down the street to have a peek at the shop Mari had mentioned.

Stepping outside the theatre, he breathed in the night air, and headed down to the old–fashioned shop. He didn't intend being out long, and hadn't bothered to put a jacket on over his shirt and waistcoat. But despite it being autumn, there wasn't a chill in the air, and he started to feel refreshed and less restless.

The craft shop was lit up and he saw a mature couple inside having fun, whatever they were up to.

Glancing up, he saw a light shining from the flat upstairs. Mari's bolthole. She'd given them her full address during their meeting. He thought he saw her near the window. Maybe she was writing another play. Or knitting. She seemed to love to do that.

During their conversation, she'd mentioned that she'd split up with her last boyfriend before she'd given up her accountancy work, and wasn't dating anyone, preferring to concentrate on making a life for herself in the city.

With no boyfriend on the scene, he pictured her working on something upstairs in her flat. Or maybe she was relaxing, unlike him, and watching a film.

She seemed a straightforward, no nonsense person, but she intrigued him. He wasn't sure why.

Shrugging away these thoughts, he walked over to peer in the window of the mysterious little shop. It was, as she'd described, and as he'd imagined. No lights on inside, so when he tried to see what it sold, there was nothing but shapes and shadows.

Feeling he'd seen all he was going to for one night, he glanced up at Mari's flat and then started to walk back up the street to the theatre.

There was a handy entrance up to his turret without having to reopen the theatre. He took this route, climbing the stairs that twisted upwards to his bolthole. On nights like this, the air felt wonderful and the view glittered with lights.

At the top of the stairs, the sky arched like a deep blue watercolour and looked close enough to reach up and touch. It was just an illusion, but he enjoyed the sense of it.

On rainy nights, and these were frequent enough, he kept a waterproof cape on hand to save himself from getting soaked. But even on windswept evenings when it was hosing down, he loved the feeling of the elements and stormy nights.

Mari finished knitting the jumper late into the night, but it had helped her unwind after the excitement of the day. The pattern had been an intricate one with cables on the front and back. A man's classic jumper. These always sold well.

She tidied her knitting away in one of the craft boxes she used to store her work. Over the years, she'd acquired a selection of pretty storage boxes, and these were arranged neatly in the living room. Her sewing basket was on the table she used as a desk where her laptop was set up, and where she wrapped her knitting parcels ready for delivery. In the basket she kept the large eye sewing needles she used to stitch the seams of the garments with yarn. It stored her pom pom maker and mending mushroom too.

Knitting needles galore were kept in a separate storage box, and she had two handy zipped holdalls for carrying her knitting with her when she was going out.

Overall, the living room retained a quietude due to the thickness of the original walls, and a historic quality, but there was no mistaking that it was occupied by a knitter. Soon to be a playwright too, hopefully.

Trying not to think how her life could change overnight if her play was accepted, she got ready for bed.

Snuggled under the covers and the patchwork quilt, she lay in bed and gazed out at the night sky, rewinding the day, even though she'd gone over it while she'd been knitting.

Telling herself that she had to get some sleep so she'd be fresh and rested for the morning, she finally drifted off.

Sunlight streamed through the windows of her flat as she sipped a cup of tea and got ready for the day. It was around ten–thirty, and she'd already got a lot done after sleeping in slightly from the late night.

Wearing a soft white jumper, again one of her own designs, she teamed it with black trousers, pumps and a neat–fitting vintage tweed jacket.

Her freshly washed and dried hair hung silkily around her shoulders and her makeup was subtle but flattering.

Planning to take the parcels downstairs to Ivy, she'd piled them up on her desk. Instead of having to take them to the post office, she had an arrangement with Ivy to add her orders to the craft shop's parcels that were picked up by courier.

As she checked her orders, a message came through on her phone from Niall.

Her heart raced as she read it:

We want to produce your play, Mari. Hope you can pop up to the theatre for elevenses.

Dancing around the little living room, bursting with joy, she took a few moments to celebrate. Finally taking a calming breath, she smoothed her hair back, grabbed her bag and laptop, gathered the parcels, along with her hopes and dreams, and hurried downstairs to the craft shop.

Having promised her customers a speedy next day delivery service, she didn't want to let them down, but the urge to leave everything and set a speed record for running up the cobbled street to the theatre was overwhelming.

Fighting against the tide of her enthusiasm, she burst into the shop, relieved to see that Ivy was busy serving a customer, thinking she could drop the parcels off and scarper without stopping to chat.

But Ivy smiled and beckoned her over. 'Oh, here's Mari, our expert knitter,' she told the customer. 'She'll know what pom pom maker is best for your pattern.'

Smiling tightly, Mari hurried over to look at the pattern the customer was eagerly showing her for a pom pom edged shawl.

Scanning the pattern, Mari knew exactly what one of the three that Ivy sold was best. 'This one is ideal.' She pointed to it on the carousel where a selection of haberdashery items were hanging.

Ivy unhooked it and put it on the counter. 'This one is on sale.'

There were smiles all round.

Thinking she could now leave, Mari went to bolt, but then she hesitated and added a tip for the customer. 'I'd recommend using a pair of small, pointed scissors to trim the wee pom poms. It'll give you a neat finish. And remember to leave a long tail on your pom poms so you can use it to secure them to your shawl.'

'I appreciate the tip,' said the customer.

Ivy smiled. 'Thanks, Mari.'

Now intent on leaving, Mari made her way to the door, but one of the members of the knitting class had walked in.

'I finished my scarf. What do you think, Mari?' The woman wore the scarf and displayed it as if posing for a photo shoot. 'I used your knitting method for keeping the edges flat. And I made a fringe like you taught me.'

'You've made a wonderful job of it,' Mari told her, genuinely pleased. 'The warm autumn colours suit you.'

Happy to have been able to show Mari her handiwork, the woman headed over to the counter to buy more yarn to knit another scarf.

Mari made her escape from the craft shop, but got waylaid by Ivy's husband as he got out of his van.

'Ah, Mari, just the lass I want to talk to.'

She tried not to let her heart sink. She liked Bob, but she was starting to panic that she'd be late for her meeting.

'I was thinking of changing the cake order for the craft classes,' he began. 'I'm going to keep the yum yums, but do you think folk would prefer jam doughnuts or do they really love the iced ones? Ivy says the iced ones go down a treat.'

'The iced doughnuts,' Mari said decisively.

'And should I add sprinkles to the icing?'

'Yes, sprinkles sound nice.'

'Vanilla or chocolate sprinkles?' He looked at her for her opinion.

'Chocolate sprinkles. You can't go wrong with chocolate,' said Mari.

He nodded firmly. 'You're right. Thanks, Mari. I'm glad I ran into you.'

And with a cheery smile, he went into the craft shop, leaving Mari a clear run up the street.

She didn't exactly run, more like a speed walk. Her flat black pumps were handy for navigating the cobbles.

Calm down, she told herself as she approached the front entrance of the theatre.

Taking a deep breath of the fresh morning air, filling her lungs, she went in, glancing at the window as she went by and seeing that the submissions notice was gone.

Niall came out of the office to greet her, and whispered quickly. 'An actor has turned up. He's in the office and is interested in the lead role in your play. Come and meet him. He's an excellent actor and played a supporting role in one of our recent plays. We'd like you to sit in on the audition.'

Mari nodded and followed Niall through to the office where Huntly was chatting to the actor.

'Mari, this is Andrew, he's going to read for us today,' Niall said, introducing them.

'Andy,' the actor said, moving like quicksilver to shake hands with her. He was so fast that she pictured sparks nearly ignited from the soles of his shoes as he skimmed across the carpet.

'Pleased to meet you,' she said, liking his open and friendly smile. He didn't have the classic handsomeness of Huntly and Niall, but his blue–green eyes had a mercurial quality that made him appear alight with energy.

Not quite as tall as them, he was around the same age, and lean and fit. His sandy blond hair was ruffled on top, he was clean–shaven, and casually dressed in jeans and a cream grandad top.

'I'm excited to talk to you about your fascinating character, Oglesby and his cat,' Andy told her.

Being thrown in at the deep end wasn't a new experience for Mari, and she adapted well to the surprise visit from the actor.

'Shall we go through to the stage so Andy can read from one of the opening scenes.' Huntly stood up and gestured through to the auditorium. He wore another clean white shirt with his waistcoat and dark trousers.

Mari noticed that a tea trolley had been set up in the office with cups, plates, napkins and a large celebratory style cake. For elevenses, she assumed, though now they'd be nearer twelve.

Huntly caught her glance. 'We always have a cake to celebrate the signing of a new play. We'll sort out all the paperwork with you later, after tea and cake. I'd have baked it myself, but I've had such a busy morning.'

Mari laughed, thinking he was joking.

'Huntly is a first class cook,' said Niall.

'So you really are adept at everything,' she remarked.

The sensual look Huntly gave her caused her heart to flutter wildly. Was he deliberately trying to make her blush?

Heading into the auditorium, such thoughts were cast aside as she saw the stage all lit up.

She was happy to be involved in the audition process, especially as this was for the leading male role of her fictitious character, Oglesby.

On stage was a mature man with a wiry build, shirt sleeves rolled up to reveal whipcord arms.

Mari frowned. Was that a stuffed toy cat he was holding?

'Peter is our prop expert,' Huntly said, introducing him to Mari. They smiled and acknowledged each other.

'I dug out Fluffy,' Peter announced to them from the stage, shaking the cat's black fur free of dust. 'He's a wee bit stoorie, and not half as fluffy as he once was, but we can brush him up until we get a better one.'

Fluffy's eyes had a glassy glint that seemed to take umbrage at being shook by the tail.

Biting her lip, Mari tried not to laugh, but was relieved when Niall guffawed.

'Poor wee kitty,' Andy sympathised, jokingly.

Then everyone laughed, and the atmosphere lifted ready for the actor's portrayal of the play's elusive Oglesby, owner of the shop that sold everything.

CHAPTER FOUR

'I'll just run to wardrobe. I'll be back in a jiffy,' said Andy, dashing off to pick up a jacket from the range of costumes on the rails.

While Andy ran away, Mari was introduced to the show's director.

Suave was the word that sprang to mind when Mari saw him walking down the centre aisle of the auditorium to join them. He wore expensive classics in neutral tones and a dark tweed jacket that made Mari look more in tune with him than the others.

'Ah, here's Jon,' said Huntly, pleased to see him. 'He's going to direct the play for us.'

Jon was of similar age and stature to Huntly and Niall, a good–looking man with light brown hair, swept back from his studious face, and pale blue eyes that preferred to cut through any nonsense. He'd become friends with them at university. A brief introduction explained that he'd agreed to direct the show they'd had to cancel, but was willing to direct the new play.

'Delighted to meet you, Mari.' Jon shook her hand and gave her a genuine smile. 'I'm intrigued by your writing. I hope I cause no offence by saying that it reminds me of playwrights of the past rather than the present. I rather like that.'

Mari was thrilled. 'I'm flattered. I've always loved classic plays, so perhaps some of that comes through in my writing.'

'A modern traditionalist,' Jon added, sounding eager to take part in the production.

Mari felt her heart racing again, but forced herself not to babble with enthusiasm.

'Here we go,' Andy said, rushing on to the stage wearing a dark blue tailcoat over his jeans and top. He straightened the front of it, tidying himself up. He'd acquired a copy of the script en route, and flipped it to the scene he was due to perform. 'I read your notes, Mari, and I think we have the same vision for Oglesby's attire. Modern vintage. Nothing anyone can pin down. A style of his own, I think you said.'

'Yes,' Mari agreed, speaking up to Andy on the stage.

'Anyone seen Fluffy?' Andy glanced around. 'Or should I say, Spindle.'

From stage left, Peter threw him the prop cat.

'Cheers,' said Andy, catching the cat and giving its fur a ruffle. 'He'll help with the piece I'm going to read for you.'

'Let's sit down.' Huntly gestured to seats three rows back from the stage.

Mari sat down with Huntly on one side and Jon on the other, while Niall took a seat beside the director.

'The cat doesn't have dialogue, is that right?' Andy called to Mari.

'Correct,' she said. 'He's not a talking cat, just a mysterious one that's glimpsed throughout the story.'

Andy smiled with relief. 'That makes it so much more dramatic.'

Sandwiched between Huntly and Jon, Mari tried to look like she was at ease with the whole situation, while Andy took a moment to get into character.

And then he began to read...

Mari watched as Andy read the dialogue, a scene near the beginning of the play when he was in his shop. His acting brought the character of Oglesby to life and she was impressed with his performance. He had a wonderful speaking voice that projected well from the stage to the auditorium, a richness that hadn't been apparent when meeting him.

She wasn't the only one impressed. Huntly, Niall and Jon were equally enthralled by Andy's portrayal, and nodded to each other that they'd found their leading man. They included Mari in their approval.

When Andy finished reading, they applauded and praised the short but dramatic performance.

'Andy would be perfect,' Huntly whispered.

'He's ideal for the role,' said Jon.

Niall agreed.

'What do you think, Mari?' Huntly said to her.

'He's an excellent actor and really captured the character,' she said.

Andy handed the cat back to Peter and then came down to join them, looking nervous but hopeful.

Huntly went over and shook Andy's hand, followed by Niall and Jon. There were smiles and chatter and Mari took a moment to take it all in, before Huntly walked back to talk to her.

'I know it's been a whirlwind for you, but Niall and I were sure that your play was for us. So we contacted those involved in the show we had to cancel.

We had to act quickly before they were committed to other plays, especially at this time of the year when seasonal shows begin hiring staff.'

'It's okay, I understand,' she assured him.

'Fortunately, everyone came back on board for this new play, and we're aiming to light a fire under it so we can launch on the opening night we'd originally planned for our autumn schedule.'

'How soon will that be?'

'As fast as we can get the show rehearsed, roles given to the actors, the scenery, props and costumes finalised.' Huntly smiled at her. 'But I just wanted to assure you that the process for your next play won't be quite so pressured.'

Mari blinked. 'My next play?'

'I don't think you're a one trick pony,' said Huntly. 'Surely you're working on your next play, or formulating it at the moment.'

'Eh, well, now that you've taken my play, I suppose I'll start working on new material. Or reworking plays that I've tucked away.'

'Do that. I'm not a playwright, but from my experience of working in this arena, I've heard that it's a great time to start putting down new ideas or revising previous plays you've written with a fresh eye.'

'I will.' She thought about the plays she'd written, not all finished, and other ideas she'd had, nothing more than scribbles. Then there was the stash of classic plays she had in one of the craft boxes. She'd started collecting plays years ago having found a bundle in a second–hand bookshop. Theatre classics, from one act scenarios to musical dramas. Studying these had helped her learn how to structure her plays. And she went to see as many live performances as she could.

'I hope the deal we've offered is suitable,' Huntly said in a confiding tone. 'But if there's anything you'd like to change or discuss, feel free. I understand you'll want time to study it.'

'I haven't received any information about the deal,' she said.

'Didn't you get my email? Niall sent a message to you this morning saying we wanted your play. Then I emailed all the details.'

Mari grabbed her phone and checked her messages. And there it was.

'I rushed here as soon as I heard from Niall,' she said, opening the attachment with the offer. 'Then I turned my phone off so I wouldn't be interrupted by knitting orders.'

As she started to read it, Huntly spoke to her.

'There's an advance of royalties we're offering. And a little extra for helping us with our leaky ship.'

'The accounting was a small favour. I wasn't looking for payment.'

'It'll save us money going forward, so we've added the extra on top of the advance for your play,' he explained.

Mari read the amount they were proposing for the advance, and gasped. 'This is very generous.'

'We think the play has the potential to be a success. When you're ready, give us your details so we can sort everything out.'

Mari's mind was still in a whirl as Niall suggested they head up to the office for tea and cake.

Jon kept pace with Huntly and Niall. Andy walked beside Mari, eager to chat to her. 'What are you writing at the moment?'

'I'm about to start something new, but I'm not sure if it'll be a play I wrote last year that I'd love to rework.'

'You'll probably view it differently now that this play has been accepted. It'll boost your confidence,' said Andy.

'Yes, everything feels like a whirlwind and I need time to relax.'

Andy laughed. 'You'll be lucky.' Then he spoke to the others. 'These guys work like blazes.'

'There's still time for tea and a slice of cake to celebrate,' said Huntly.

They all poured into the office and Huntly flicked the kettle on to boil while serving up slices of the three layer vanilla sponge cake, filled with strawberry jam and cream, that was covered with rich, buttercream icing and decorated with white chocolate curls.

Mari noticed the name on the napkins that had come with the cake delivery. 'I see that Ivy's husband baked this.' She explained that Ivy owned the craft shop and that her husband was a baker.

'It's a big small world,' said Huntly, pouring their tea. They helped themselves to milk and sugar.

There were four chairs, so one short, and Huntly parked himself on the side of the desk while the others sat around it.

The intimate and informal celebration made Mari feel that she could be part of this world. It was a dream come true. But that's what writing her play was all about. Creating a dream world that people could enjoy while they were in the audience. Now she was one of the team.

'We'll give you a proper tour of the theatre after we've had our cake,' said Huntly.

'I'd like to walk through some ideas I have with Mari,' Jon added. 'Up on the stage, so you can get a feel for what I have in mind.'

Andy was keen to join them.

'And you'll meet Sammy, our set director,' Huntly said to Mari. 'He's made some astounding sets for us before, and has decades of experience in the business.'

Mari had just eaten a mouthful of the delicious cake. 'Great,' she mumbled, causing them to laugh.

The light atmosphere helped her realise that this was actually going ahead and in the not too distant future the theatre would be filled with an audience eager to watch the play she'd written.

A message came through on Niall's phone. He ignored it. Then another message, and another, until he sighed and checked what was so urgent that it merited interrupting their celebration.

Whatever it was, Niall frowned and then glanced at Huntly. 'Red alert.'

Huntly sighed, and put his plate down on the desk, as if he'd lost his appetite to finish the remainder of his cake.

Mari's expression made Huntly sigh again, and he explained the incoming warning. 'Scarlet is on her way to the theatre.'

It transpired through the three of them chipping in details about Scarlet, none of them thrilled at the prospect of her arriving, that Scarlet was an actress and model seeking a part in the new play. But the main role it seemed she was after was as Huntly's girlfriend.

'I'm not interested in dating Scarlet,' Huntly made this quite clear to Mari. The others seemed to know the intricacies of Scarlet's wiles.

'Have you made this clear to her?' said Mari.

'Yes,' Huntly explained. 'But it creates an awkward situation. I've tried to be fair and offered her a role in one of our previous shows. That's when the trouble began. She became a disruptive element to the rest of the cast and those involved in the show.'

'I've never been enamoured with her acting,' said Jon, enjoying his tea and cake. 'She's stunningly beautiful, but cold as winter. She's done quite well for herself I suppose in a couple of dramatic productions, but she's certainly not right for this play.'

Andy didn't say anything, but from his tense expression, Mari surmised he wasn't keen to work with her either.

Breaking the tension, Peter popped his head round the office door. 'I've got a great idea for Fluffy.'

Everyone listened to the prop manager's suggestion.

'I'm going to stick batteries up his bahookie,' said Peter. 'And stuff a mechanism in him that will make it look like he's breathing when he's sitting on set.'

'That sounds creepy,' said Huntly. 'Give it a go though.'

'Will do,' and off he went to work on the prop cat.

Andy spoke up. 'Sammy the set director told me he's planning to create an effect with the lighting to make it look like the cat is a slinky shadow prowling across the back of the stage.'

'That could look amazing,' said Mari. In a part of the play she'd written a note suggesting that the shadow of the cat was cast against the night glow of the city. Clearly, the set director had read this and was going to try to create it.

'It's a pity you can't use your theatre cat,' Jon commented, wiping the buttercream off his fingers on to a napkin. 'But you couldn't possibly use a real cat.'

'We don't have a cat,' Huntly told him casually.

Jon looked surprised and thumbed towards the office door. 'There was a lovely black cat sitting outside the theatre entrance when I arrived. It looked at me with these vibrant green eyes as I walked past.' He glanced at Mari. 'Its eyes were even more curious and green than yours, Mari.'

Everyone except Mari shrugged away the thought of them having a theatre cat.

Could it be Spindle, she wondered, and then dismissed this until Jon made another comment.

'When I glanced back to see if the cat was following me into the theatre, it had gone,' said Jon.

'Probably looking for tasty scraps,' Andy suggested.

Niall put his empty plate down on the desk. 'Or knew we had cake.'

Smiling, and drinking down their tea, they piled their plates on to the tea tray.

'Right, let's give you a proper tour of the theatre,' Huntly said to Mari.

'Remember, I'm stealing Mari for a chat about the stage directions,' Jon reminded Huntly lightly.

Chatting about what they were planning to do, things to be done, Mari was swept along in the liveliness of their company and into the heart of the theatre.

'The stage is higher than I imagined,' Mari commented, standing up on it, looking out at all the empty seats that would be filled with the audience.

'It's quite deceiving,' said Jon. 'Actors are accustomed to it, and some stages are higher than others, but this one is a nice height and there's a great atmosphere in this theatre even when it's just us here.'

Mari felt the sense of excitement. She turned to Andy. 'I've seen lots of plays, but this is the first time I've ever stood on stage.'

'It gives you a whole different perspective, doesn't it,' said Andy, coming over and pointing at the seats. 'I love seeing the faces of the audience react as they enjoy a show. Though depending on the lighting, I can only glimpse those near the front. But I can sense the reactions, like waves washing towards me when I'm up on the stage performing.'

'I'd never have the talent or the confidence to act on stage like you do, Andy,' said Mari.

Andy leaned close. 'And I can't write for toffee. So thankfully each person to their own talents.'

'Exactly,' Jon chimed–in. 'So let's talk about how we're going to portray this fascinating shop that sells everything and really capture the audience's imagination.'

As everyone buzzed around, Mari took her tweed jacket off and hung it on a chair at the side of the stage. The pretty white jumper showed her slender curves, though she was unaware that she'd caught Huntly's attention.

From down near the middle row of seats, Huntly admired how lovely Mari looked, then forced such thoughts away, reminding himself of his own rule not to get involved with anyone working on the show. But still, he couldn't help liking Mari, and the depth of the attraction took him off guard.

Jumping up on to the stage to join Mari, Jon and Andy, he approached her and pointed up towards the back of the auditorium.

'That's the control box up there,' Huntly told her. It looked like a small room, like that for a cinema projector, tucked away so it didn't obscure the audience's view. 'Our set director, Sammy, is adjusting the lighting and trying out different effects. During the show, the lighting and sound is controlled from there.'

Mari was enjoying taking in the information given to her, starting to see how they planned all the aspects of the show to fit together into the finished performance. Sitting in many different theatres, she'd never had a peek behind the scenes to see the workings, like a spider's web of creativity, being spun into a play for the audience to watch.

Huntly waved up to Sammy. Dimming the lighting inside the control box so they could see him better, Sammy waved back.

His white hair and beard reminded her of Santa Claus, and she raised her hand to acknowledge the set director when he included her in his wave.

Flicking the lighting system back up, Sammy fiddled with the control panel, adjusting the magnification on something he was working on, and shone a beam of light on to the back of the stage.

The shadow of a huge black cat appeared to slink along, causing Andy to shriek when he saw it behind him.

'Jings!' Andy gasped and then laughed.

'Sorry, Andy,' Sammy announced over the microphone. 'Got my magnification mixed up a wee bit.'

Everyone was laughing.

'A wee bit,' said Andy, pretending to calm his heart. 'I thought someone had been overfeeding Fluffy.'

In all the merriment, a lot of practical work was done, including Mari learning the specific names for the main areas on stage so that she'd know what Jon and others were talking about.

'The crossover is the hidden walkway just behind the stage where actors and crew can cross from one side to the other without the audience seeing them,' Jon explained.

'We store scenery backdrops and props there too,' Peter the prop manager told her while wiring up the cat's bahookie.

'Sometimes the backdrops look like a pack of cards with backgrounds lined up to be interchanged during the show,' Andy added.

'Any suggestions for the actual shop,' said Huntly. 'In my mind, it sort of looks like the curious old shop down the street.'

Jon's interest perked up. 'What shop is that?'

'It's the one that helped me picture the shop in my play,' said Mari. 'The one in my play is fictional, but as I was writing the scenes, I imagined what a mysterious shop would feel like.'

'Is Oglesby the owner of the real shop?' Andy said to her.

'No, the name is fiction too,' Mari told him. She explained about Ivy not even knowing much about the elusive owner of the shop opposite her craft shop. 'Everyone seems to describe the owner differently. But I made up what I pictured the character would look like.'

'I like your depiction,' said Andy. 'It's a terrific role, with layers of mystery and a touch of magic, and things not entirely explainable.'

'That's what intrigued me when I read the first act,' Jon added.

Huntly agreed.

'What about the cat?' said Jon. 'Is there a real Spindle?'

'Yes and no,' Mari replied. 'There's a black cat with green eyes that appears from time to time near the shop that's always closed. As if he's the owner's cat. But no one is sure. Ivy said that one day she was outside her craft shop talking to a customer about spindles, small wooden spindles used for hand spinning your own yarn for knitting.'

She showed them a picture of a drop spindle on her phone, then continued to explain.

'Anyway, Ivy said that when she mentioned the word spindle, the cat reacted, as if that was his name,' said Mari. 'Ivy tried other names from Twinkle to Thimble, but to no effect. So although no one knows what the cat's real name is, he's become Spindle. So I used that name for Oglesby's cat.'

'It's perfect,' said Jon.

Mari wondered if Jon would then mention about the black cat outside the theatre, but the conversation changed to discussing how they'd create the shop for the stage setting.

Huntly, Mari and Jon went back down to the front seats leaving Andy on stage.

Jon described what he had in mind for the opening scene, gesturing up to the stage, his tone filled with enthusiasm. 'I picture that the establishing scene will have the shop aglow at night...lights shining through the old–fashioned windows, the cat sitting inside, and stars twinkling in the sky...'

Niall's phone began to light up with messages again, and he threw Huntly a warning look. Another red alert, Mari rightly assumed. Only this time, Scarlet was in the theatre.

Before Huntly could plan a course of action or evasion, Scarlet was walking down the centre aisle, as if strutting on a fashion runway in towering black heels, and a tight–fitting black top and figure–hugging black skirt. Her beauty was as cold as Jon had described, but with her shoulder–length dark hair and porcelain skin, there was no ignoring the statuesque model–actress.

Scarlet walked towards Huntly, but cast a daggered glance at Mari.

Huntly instinctively stepped closer to Mari, ready to shield her from any barbed remarks.

Mari saw the challenging look in Scarlet's ice grey eyes, but it wasn't the colour she noticed most, it was the feeling they gave her. And sensed the trouble brewing.

CHAPTER FIVE

'We're rehearsing our new play. You can't be here,' Huntly told Scarlet. Firm, but polite.

'You always had a talent for being blunt, Huntly.' Scarlet's confidence didn't dip. 'But I'm here to be part of your new show. Everyone's talking about it.'

'There isn't a part for you.' Huntly's deep voice resonated in the theatre.

Scarlet smiled, undaunted, and stepped closer to him. 'Oh, don't be silly, there has to be a part for me, even a small role.'

Jon was having none of Scarlet's nonsense and spoke up. 'This play has less characters than the previous one. We've given every part to actors assigned to the other play.'

Scarlet was less inclined to argue with the director, and forced a smile. 'Well, I've been offered a part in another show, a rival production.' She shrugged. 'I wanted to give you the chance to invite me to join your play, but I suppose I'll be accepting the other offer.'

'Do that,' said Jon.

Huntly nodded. He didn't want to engage in further conversation with her, hoping she'd leave quietly. But his hopes were dashed when she deigned to look at Mari.

'You must be the little knitter.' Scarlet's tone was deliberately snide.

Huntly was about to verbally defend Mari, but it wasn't necessary. Mari's reply was instant.

'I'm not taking any knitting orders today,' Mari said, facing up to Scarlet. 'But if you're looking for a nice new cardigan or a shawl, I can recommend the craft shop down the street. You'll find all the latest fashionable colours for the autumn to brighten up your sombre black ensemble. And there's a sale on.' Mari finished with a pleasant smile.

The heated atmosphere dropped to the ice cold mark. Scarlet blinked, taken aback by Mari's response.

Mari saw the whites of Huntly's eyes as he glanced at her, trying not to flinch, while inwardly cheering her on.

Niall stifled a grin.

Scarlet had another run at Mari, sounding indignant. 'Do I look like I would wear an old-fashioned woollen shawl?'

Mari shrugged. 'From the cold atmosphere you brought in with you, maybe you could benefit from it.'

Andy guffawed from the stage, unable to contain his laughter.

Scarlet glared up at him. 'Good luck being part of this amateur's play, Andy.'

Andy held up Fluffy. 'Thank you, Scarlet, but luckily I have a black cat.'

Scarlet stared icy daggers at Mari.

'I'll see you out,' Niall said to Scarlet.

'I can see myself out.' Scarlet strutted away, but Niall escorted her anyway.

Jon clasped his hands together and took a deep breath. 'So, where were we? Ah, yes, stars twinkling in the night sky.'

Everyone knew how the situation had unfolded, pushed aside the interruption, and continued where they'd left off. The residue of Scarlet's visit lingered for a few minutes, and then the temperature in the theatre started to warm up again.

Huntly put his hand on Mari's arm and whispered to her. 'I apologise for Scarlet's attitude. I know this is your first play, but I don't think of you as an amateur.'

'Thank you, Huntly,' Mari said softly.

No more was said about it, and Jon beckoned Mari back up on to the stage. Jon referenced her description of a scene. 'I think we can add to the atmosphere of the cobbled street with lantern lights, while Andy enters from stage left.'

Mari read the part that Jon was meaning, and nodded. 'Yes, that would be great.'

Huntly watched Mari and Jon working well together, and felt assured that he'd picked the right team to create a show that audiences would enjoy. Jon was a first–class director, as well as a long–time friend, and Mari was willing to throw herself into the heart of the production, learning the process quickly. He admired her writing talent, and found himself liking her too. And again, that feeling of attraction touched his heart, but he knew there was no place for romance in the midst of all the work they had to do.

Niall came back in, jokingly touching the tip of his nose, pretending to check that it was still there. 'Scarlet had a few things to say to me before she left the theatre.' He didn't sound surprised or upset. 'Do you think she'll still try to cause trouble for us?'

'She's Scarlet,' said Huntly. 'I doubt we've seen the last of her.'

'Huntly,' Jon called to him. 'We'd love to have a starry night sky effect when Oglesby is getting ready to lock up his shop for the evening.'

Huntly joined them on stage. 'Is that where he sees our heroine walking away after she's bought an old book in his shop?'

'Yes,' said Jon. 'But then he notices from the window that she's been followed by two dubious characters and heads out to rescue her.'

As they continued to map out ideas for the play, Heather, the wardrobe manager, came hurrying on to the stage and thrust a vintage waistcoat at Andy.

'Look what I found,' said Heather. In her forties, she had auburn hair pinned up in a messy bun, and an enthusiasm for fashion and creating stage costumes. Her spectacles dangled from a beaded chain around her neck, and she wore colourful separates that suited her bright character.

Andy's face lit up. 'You found it!' He grabbed the waistcoat, took his jacket off, and put the waistcoat on. 'I knew I'd seen it somewhere.'

'It was hanging up on the rails,' Heather told him, pleased that she'd located it.

Andy then put the jacket on over the waistcoat. 'An ideal match for the jacket. Thanks, Heather.'

'I'll get you kitted out with one of the vintage shirts and trousers,' Heather told Andy, and then as she went to walk away she saw Mari talking to Huntly and Jon.

'Mari!' Heather exclaimed. 'So it's true, you wrote the play.' She came hurrying over.

'I didn't know you worked in the theatre,' said Mari, pleased to see her, but surprised.

'I go to Mari's knitting classes at the craft shop,' Heather explained to the others. 'She's taught me how to improve my intarsia knitting,' she said, referring to the technique to knit different colours of yarn into a pattern. 'My colourwork is so much neater now.'

'Heather is our wardrobe manager,' said Huntly, happy that the women knew each other.

Mari knew Heather from the class, but didn't know her occupation.

'Are you still going to teach your knitting classes at the shop?' Heather wanted to know. An expert seamstress and dressmaker, she'd wanted to improve her knitting and joined the classes when she'd seen them advertised in the craft shop.

'Yes,' Mari assured her. 'I'm continuing with my knitting while working on the play.'

'You're going to be a busy bee,' Heather said, smiling. 'Okay, I won't keep you back from your work.' And with a cheery wave, Heather hurried away to the wardrobe area in search of more outfits for the cast.

'What are you going to do about your knitting work?' Jon said to Mari.

'Juggle the two,' Mari replied. 'Everything's happened in such a whirlwind, I haven't had time to think about it. But I don't plan to stop knitting.' She glanced at Huntly, hoping he agreed.

'This is a hectic day,' said Huntly. 'And there will be plenty of those. But between those, there will be ample time for you to continue your knitting work at the shop and in your own time. And you're welcome to bring your knitting with you to the theatre if you want.'

Mari looked at Huntly for clarity. 'That would be okay?'

'Yes,' Huntly said firmly.

Jon agreed. 'Often there's a lot of sitting around while scenery is changed and we go over the dialogue with the actors.'

'And you won't need to be here every day,' Huntly added. 'Your time will be flexible. But we'll need you to collaborate with Jon, rewrite dialogue if needed, help to rework scenes.'

'I'm happy to spend as much time here at the theatre as necessary,' said Mari. 'I want to be involved. But if I can bring my knitting with me, that would be handy.'

Agreeing to this plan, they all got on with working on ideas to get the production started on a tight schedule.

Steeped in the windowless theatre, it was easy for time to drift by, and soon the afternoon became early evening.

Mari had enjoyed being involved in the planning of the production and was fired up on the energy of it all.

Huntly checked the time. 'I think we should call it a day and have dinner.'

Niall and Jon agreed.

Jon clasped a copy of the play. 'We can discuss the second act over dinner and decide if we want to create a snowy atmosphere at the end of act one.'

Thinking that she'd be heading back to her flat, Mari put her jacket on and picked up her bag. Her laptop was tucked inside it.

But they were planning to go to one of their favourite restaurants nearby — and Mari was invited too.

Huntly took out his phone. 'I'll book a table for four.'

Andy was going on a dinner date with his girlfriend to celebrate landing the leading role in the play, and left, saying he'd see them again the following day.

The set director turned off the lights in the control box and waved goodnight to Huntly.

Huntly waved and nodded to Sammy.

It seemed to be standard practice for Huntly to secure the theatre at night as he often stayed upstairs in his turret, or worked late into the evenings there.

Everyone from Heather to the prop manager had left the theatre by the time Mari, Huntly, Niall and Jon headed to the restaurant.

Outside the theatre, Mari breathed in the early evening. The sky was streaked with bands of lilac and pink, slowly fading into the deep blue of the night.

They walked to the restaurant, chatting all the way, taking a shortcut through one of the many alleyways that trailed off from the cobbled street. Up a few steps and then down others, they were soon at the restaurant that had a welcoming glow.

Huntly and the others were greeted by staff, knowing them well, and they were shown to their reserved table and handed menus.

The establishment was upmarket, and Mari eyed the wonderful selection of dishes on the menu. She opted for a traditional dinner with roast potatoes and rich gravy. Jon joined her, while Huntly and Niall had the baked salmon with herbs, lemon slices and vegetables. Huntly added cranberry sauce to his order, while Niall preferred a butter sauce.

Mari was seated opposite Huntly, and while they chatted about the play, he found it hard not to admire her. He started to wish he hadn't curtailed himself by his own rules, but he knew it was better not to complicate things.

'I think we should introduce the snow scenes after we've opened with a rich, autumn atmosphere,' said Jon. 'What do you think, Mari?'

'I agree.' This is how she'd written it. 'I wasn't sure when I was writing the first act whether my ideas for creating a wintry atmosphere would be difficult to achieve. I added in my notes that I'd love to start with one of those gorgeous autumn nights when shops haven't yet put up their Christmas decorations, but there's a feeling of winter in the air.'

'We can create that,' Huntly assured her. 'But I like that the play starts on a late afternoon in the autumn, with lights starting to flicker and shops getting ready to close for the day. And by the end of the first act, we have the snow.'

'Sammy is an amazing set director,' said Niall.

'The cat prowling in the background is going to be terrific,' Jon added.

Mari ate her dinner and let the conversation flow around her, still having moments when she had to pinch herself that she was actually having her play performed.

'We'll need blurb to start promoting the play,' said Huntly. 'Would you be able to come up with a few paragraphs summarising the story, Mari?'

The three of them looked hopefully at her.

'I could jot down something if it helps,' Jon offered. 'But it's better if the writer describes the storyline of the play.'

'I'll have a go at writing it,' said Mari. 'I've read the synopses of plays advertising and promoting them in magazines, so I'll put together something.'

Huntly admired that Mari was willing to have a go at whatever was needed.

'We'll use it to update the theatre's website,' said Huntly. 'Word is already getting around that we're preparing to produce a new play, so we'll describe the story before the gossip catches fire.'

'We're aiming for an initial run of the play,' Niall explained. 'But if it's a roaring success, we'll extend the run as necessary.'

'It won't be on every evening,' Jon added. 'But it will be our lead play along with our other shows from our original schedule that was cast to the wind.'

'And Wil hasn't ruled out putting on an evening of his new dance show,' said Huntly.

'I'd love to see everything on your schedule,' said Mari.

'Tickets are a perk of working with us,' Huntly told her with a warm smile.

'You'll see Wil rehearsing his dance routines at the theatre soon,' Niall explained to her.

'Another perk,' Mari said chirpily.

'Do you dance?' Jon said to her.

'No, not at all.' Except when dancing around her flat celebrating her play being accepted.

'Most of us dance for fun,' said Jon. 'Though some of us have other hidden talents. Like Huntly, with his talent for playing the piano, and that's something I do envy.'

Mari looked at Huntly. 'Do you play the baby grand piano that's in the theatre?'

Before Huntly could reply, Jon spoke up. 'Plays it like a maestro. He's classically trained since he was a wee boy.'

'Do you ever perform on stage?' Mari said to Huntly.

'Never. I play for fun, for pleasure,' Huntly stated firmly.

'We've tried to persuade him, but to no avail,' said Jon.

'Niall plays guitar, acoustic and electric.' Huntly tried to put the spotlight on him.

'Truly for fun,' said Niall.

'I can't even ting a triangle in time,' Jon joked. 'But these two are back–up if any of our shows go awry. It's a shame you don't dance, Mari. I'm quite light on my feet. I could've waltzed you around the stage while Huntly played us a concerto.'

'Your ex–girlfriend was less than complementary about your dance moves at our last after show party,' Niall reminded Jon.

Jon guffawed. 'She grumbled about everything I did.'

The jovial conversation continued as their puddings were served. Mari had a hot chocolate sundae, Huntly preferred sticky toffee pudding, Niall wanted apple and bramble crumble with custard, while Jon ordered a strawberry and meringue confection topped with whipped cream.

Mari gazed out at the view from the window, seeing the lilac glow in the sky disappear into the inky hues as the evening wore on.

Huntly finally settled the bill and they headed out into the night. The warmth of the day lingered well, but there was a definite sense of autumn in the night air.

'I'm parked that way.' Jon nodded further along the street.

Niall was parked in another direction.

'I can find my way home,' said Mari. 'It's less than a ten minute walk, and I love strolling through Edinburgh on evenings like this.' She shrugged her bag up on to her shoulder ready to walk away.

'I'll walk you back,' Huntly insisted. 'I'm heading to the theatre, so it's on my route.' This was true, but he wanted to walk her home.

Waving to each other, they parted ways, and Mari found herself walking along the cobbled streets with

Huntly, talking about the play and about her life in general.

'What about your family,' he said. 'Do your parents stay in the coastal town?'

'No, they're gone, so I'm on my own and have been for several years,' she told him.

'I'm sorry.'

'It's okay. I manage. And now look what I'm doing. Living in Edinburgh, knitting and involved in the theatre.' She smiled up at him. He was so tall as he walked beside her.

'My parents travel a lot to Europe and abroad,' he said. 'They're enjoying their travels, but the past few years we haven't seen much of each other.'

'Do they approve of you running the theatre?'

'Yes, and so do Niall's parents, but all our lives are so busy.'

As they walked towards the craft shop, Huntly looked up at the darkened windows of her flat, remembering seeing the lights on the previous night. The craft shop was closed and opposite them the old–fashioned shop was in darkness too.

Mari slowed down as she approached the close at the side of the craft shop. A dim light lit the entrance through to the stairs that led up to her flat.

'I'll walk you to your door,' Huntly insisted.

Heading through the close and up the stone steps, Mari jiggled the key in the lock and opened her front door, expecting Huntly to turn and leave.

'I must buy one or two of your jumpers,' he said, glancing around him. 'The autumn nights will be colder soon.' He looked as if he could sense it in the air. 'Are they on your website, or for sale in the craft shop?'

'Both. I've been knitting a few men's jumpers. A traditional Aran knit, a Fair Isle style and a classic winter grey design.'

'Do you design your own patterns?'

'Yes, I love creating my own designs, and men's jumpers are popular with my customers, especially at this time of year.'

'Save a couple for me. I'd really like to buy them. I wear jumpers every winter and could do with some new ones.'

Before she could think through the consequences of her invitation, she gestured for Huntly to come in. 'I've finished a few jumpers if you want to pop in for a minute to see if they suit you.'

Huntly nodded, eager to accept her invitation to come in. He genuinely wanted to buy the jumpers, but he was interested to take a peek inside Mari's flat. To see a glimpse of her world.

CHAPTER SIX

Huntly followed Mari inside the flat. His tall, broad shouldered, masculine stature seemed to fill it, highlighted in the night glow that streamed like silver through the windows.

She turned a lamp on, put her bag down and went over to where the jumpers were neatly folded.

Huntly glanced around the little flat. The crafted items created a homeliness, from the crocheted blanket on the couch to the pretty appliqué cushions. The bedroom door was open and he glimpsed the patchwork quilt on the bed. 'This is cosy.'

'I like it. And as I said, the view is wonderful.'

Huntly went over to the window and peered out, seeing a view of the city that was a variation of the one he had from his turret.

'You probably have an outstanding view of Edinburgh from above the theatre,' she said.

'I do. But this view is beautiful.' The city glittered as if sprinkled with starlight. He glanced up at the night sky. 'And look at the stars.'

Mari stood beside Huntly, and for a moment they shared the view.

The thickness of the walls shut out the world, and in the quietude she wondered if he could hear the excited beating of her heart.

A starry night together to remember, she thought, before stepping back from the temptation of Huntly.

'These are the jumpers,' she said, showing him her latest designs.

Huntly lifted each one up and held them in front of himself. 'Would you mind if I try them on? I know it's late.'

'Help yourself. See how they feel when you wear them.'

He took his waistcoat off and put the Aran knit on over his shirt.

'I love this,' he said.

Mari checked that the sleeves were the right length and the shoulders were a comfortable fit. She nodded. 'It fits you well.'

'I'll buy it.' And then he tried on the Fair Isle.

Again, Mari checked that it fitted him. 'These are all a medium to large size, but I like to make them slightly generous so they're comfy to wear over a shirt or tee.'

'This feels so comfy, I don't want to take it off.' But he did, so he could try on the grey jumper.

'You suit the grey too,' she said, reaching up to check that it sat well on his shoulders. And for a moment, she met his gaze as he looked down at her. The look in those fabulous sapphire eyes of his melted her heart.

Huntly sensed the spark of attraction between them, and fought the urge to lean down and claim her sweet lips with his.

Mari stepped back, pretending she hadn't sensed the burning passion that had ignited between them.

Huntly feigned more interest in the jumpers than in Mari. 'Can I take these with me?'

'What, all three jumpers?'

'If they're for sale.' He was still wearing the grey one.

'They are.'

Mari put them in a bag along with his waistcoat.

He insisted on making the payment there and then, online to her website.

'I see that you've got your own label sewn into the jumpers,' he remarked.

'Yes, I stitch them into all the garments I knit.'

Then he noticed one of her wooden drop spindles on the table beside a bundle of wool fibres and recognised it from the picture she'd shown to him earlier.

He put his bag down and picked it up, eyeing it from all angles. 'I can't fathom how you'd spin your own wool with this.'

Mari took the spindle off him, lifted up the bundle of wool and gave him a brief demonstration. 'There's a little hook at the top of the spindle that I use to attach the wool fibres, teasing them out gently so that they twist clockwise around the spindle into a single strand of yarn.'

Huntly watched, fascinated as the yarn was spun in front of him.

'Do you want to try it?' she offered. 'It's a bit fiddly until you get the hang of it. But it's fun to spin your own yarn.'

'I'll give it a go,' he said, letting her take charge of his hands, showing him how to tease the fibres with his fingers, and then smiled as the spindle started to spin a thin strand.

'You really are annoyingly good at everything, aren't you,' she said playfully.

Huntly smiled. 'No, I'm all bluff and thunder.'

'That's not true,' she argued lightly. 'Even Niall and Jon think you are.'

'They're biased.'

Mari shook her head, and watched as he continued to spin a bit more yarn. 'If I ever need a hand to help me spin yarn, I'll give you a call.'

'You can always call me,' he said, with an extra hint of something she wasn't sure of, but it caused that fluttering in her heart again.

He handed her back the spindle.

She tied the long strand of yarn he'd spun into a tidy sample and gave it to him. 'Here's a keepsake of your first hand spun piece of yarn.'

Huntly clasped it and smiled. 'Thank you. I will keep this.' To remember the exciting day they'd had, and the evening, culminating in him being here with her in the flat, learning to spin yarn late at night when the rest of the sensible world was tucked up in bed.

As she put the spindle away in one of her craft boxes, he noticed the box filled with the plays she'd collected.

'I love reading original plays, and books about plays,' she explained. 'I've collected a few.'

He nodded, impressed. And then glanced around. 'Do you write in here, on your own, or do you sit in cafes, or outdoors when the weather is fine?'

'I write everything in here. I prefer to work on my own where it's quiet. I don't even like background music when I'm writing.'

'I'm not a writer, but I can understand you wanting calm and quiet to work. I prefer to think things through at the end of a long, busy day, at home. Though I do love to cook,' he admitted. 'That helps me to unwind, and there's the benefit of eating a tasty dinner.'

'I can cook, but it's nothing too fancy. Just plain, old–fashioned, cooking.'

'There's nothing better than a home cooked meal and great company to share it with.' Don't do it, he instantly urged himself. Do not invite her to have dinner. 'Let me cook dinner for you one evening. The kitchen upstairs from the theatre is kitted out for cooking various cuisine.'

Mari blinked. Was he inviting her to have a romantic dinner with him?

Her look made him realise he should've listened to himself. 'As friends, nothing more. No kissing clauses or anything like that.' Jeez, he thought, get a grip. He sounded like a total fool.

'Okay.'

That one word of acceptance saved him from nose diving into deeper trouble.

'Great. We'll arrange an evening to suit us both.' He hoped his tone sounded nonchalant.

Mari wondered if she'd misconstrued his kind offer to cook dinner. She shook the other thoughts away. Huntly was just being friendly, and after all, they were going to be working closely together on the play.

Huntly checked the time. 'Right, I think we should get to bed now.'

Mari's mind flipped, and she stared wide–eyed at him.

'What I mean is,' he corrected himself, wishing he could rewind his remark, 'it's late. I should go and let you get some sleep.' He headed for the door, taking the bag of jumpers with him. 'See you tomorrow around the same time.'

'For elevenses,' she said, smiling.

'That usually ends up being nearer twelve.'

Smiling at her with that sensual grin, Huntly left the flat wearing the grey jumper and with his waistcoat tucked into the bag with the other two new purchases.

Mari locked the door after he'd gone, and then couldn't resist peering out the front window, watching him walk along the cobbled street.

Sensing her watching, or hoping she was there, Huntly glanced up at the window, waved, and walked away into the night.

He heard his footsteps on the cobbles in the quiet of the evening, and felt the autumn air try and fail to get through his new, cosy jumper. There was something extra about the feel of it. Not just the soft yarn in shades of grey, or the intricate texture of the pattern, like cables entwined on the front of it. But knowing that Mari had knitted it brought a special quality that he couldn't quite define. Or didn't want to, for it could only lead to him developing feelings for her that wouldn't work out. Mari had been wrong when she said he was good at everything. The one thing that mattered most was his greatest failure — romance. Finding true love was as elusive as the magical elements she'd woven into her play.

Reaching the theatre, he headed up to the turret.

He kept the main lights and lamps off, and got ready for bed by the glow of the twinkle lights that were draped around the windows' panoramic views.

He put his new jumpers away in the wardrobe, then stripped off and put on a pair of grey silk bottoms. Standing for a moment gazing out at the glittering cityscape, he thought he saw a black cat sitting on a distant rooftop looking over at him. In the blink of an eye, it had gone.

Putting it down to all the talk of the play's mysterious cat, Huntly got into bed, pulled the covers up and fell asleep.

The night sky was particularly bright with stars, and Mari lay in bed gazing out the window, rewinding the events of the day, and the evening, particularly the part where Huntly was in her flat.

Planning the most efficient way to organise the following day, she drifted off to sleep.

In the depths of the night she woke up, her mind alert with ideas of what to write for the play's synopsis.

Sitting up in bed, she flicked the lamp on, grabbed the notepad and pen she kept on her bedside table, and began scribbling it down. Maybe when she read it in the morning, it would be nothing more than midnight meanderings, but hopefully it would give her rough notes she could tidy up into the synopsis.

She was sure that Huntly and the others didn't expect her to write something overnight, but it would be handy to be able to give them a rough outline for their initial approval.

As the storyline took shape on the paper, she glanced again out the window at the starry sky, thinking that here she was in the city, writing into the night, before turning the light off and snuggling down again.

Blinking awake to the sound of her early morning alarm, she sat up and grabbed the notepad, hoping the scribbles made sense.

A deep breath of relief washed over her. They were rough, but coherent.

Throwing back the covers, she jumped into her slippers and scurried through to her laptop where she sat down and started to type everything she'd written, tidying up the synopsis. She added to it with a fresh eye, changed a paragraph around, and before she'd showered or had breakfast, the synopsis was done.

Mentally punching the air that the pressure of that task had lifted, she got showered and dressed ready to start her busy day. Beginning with a mug of tea and hot buttered toast.

She wore a soft pink jumper with her cinnamon cords and comfy pumps, and popped downstairs to the craft shop with her parcels for posting to customers, wondering how Ivy would react when she told her the news about her play.

Pretty bunting fluttered in the bright morning breeze, but as she was used to Ivy's lovely window displays, she didn't think anything of it. Two crochet cats, one knitted cushion cat and a quilted kitty sat inside along with a colourful selection of yarn and fat quarter bundles of fabric for crafts and quilting.

Mari walked in with her parcels and was greeted with cheering and clapping from Ivy.

Hurrying round from behind the counter, Ivy grabbed the parcels off her, put them down with the others for collection, and then beamed the biggest smile at Mari.

'Well done, Mari!' Ivy then smothered her in a hug.

Mari wasn't sure what the extra warm welcome was for, but then it became clear.

'Heather told me about your play,' Ivy said, looking thrilled. 'That's marvellous. I didn't know you were a secret playwright.'

'I've been working on my writing for a while. I never thought I'd have this play performed at the theatre. I'm still pinching myself with the whole whirlwind of excitement.'

'No wonder,' Ivy agreed. She clicked her fingers. 'I heard that Huntly and Niall snapped up your play as soon as they read it. And Heather says you're working with them in the theatre now.'

'I am, but I'm still going to be doing my knitting, and taking the classes.'

'Yes, Heather mentioned that too.'

'I'll be taking my knitting with me to the theatre and working on it between the rehearsals for the play.'

'It's so handy to be able to juggle both. And I'll help wiggle your schedule around the play commitments,' Ivy assured her. 'What a wonderful new career path. A playwright!'

'I'm still not used to that title, and not sure if I merit it yet.'

'Oh, hush, that's silly talk. Heather says the play's going full steam ahead.'

'It is. I'm due up at the theatre for eleven this morning.'

The shop door opened wide and in walked Bob, carrying a large celebration cake. The same type he'd made and delivered to the theatre, only this one had white chocolate curls and raspberry jam filling.

'Stand aside, girls. Make way for the cake.'

Laughing, Mari and Ivy stepped back as Bob put the cake down on the counter.

Ivy ran through to the back kitchen and put the kettle on for tea, calling through to them. 'We couldn't let news like this go by without a wee celebration.'

Bob gave Mari a bear hug. 'Well done, lass. We're delighted for you.'

'Thank you, you're so kind.' Mari felt herself well up.

The front door burst open again, this time with several members of Mari's knitting class, including Heather, and other customers from the craft shop.

Under a blanket of cuddles and congratulations, tea and cake was served up, and the cheery chatter circled around Mari, with everyone sharing in the excitement.

Lots of photos were taken and these were due to be put up on the craft shop website.

The whirlwind of publicity had started, Mari realised amid the melee.

Heather nudged Mari. 'Huntly seems quite taken with you.'

Ivy picked up on this snippet. 'Oooh! The handsome Huntly. Is there romance in the air?'

Before Mari could respond, Heather replied. 'Definitely, but I think he's trying not to overstep the mark with our Mari.'

The others were all keen to hear the details.

Mari tried to tame the gossip. 'Huntly's been a total gentleman. Generous and kind.'

'Well, I think there are sparks between you,' said Heather.

There were giggles and gossip, and somewhere in it all, Mari let slip that she'd invited Huntly up to her flat to try on the jumpers.

Lots more giggles and playful comments rippled around the shop, and even Mari laughed amid her blushing.

'Huntly has a firm rule not to get involved romantically with anyone he works with,' Mari told them.

Heather smiled knowingly. 'Huntly's always been a rule breaker.'

'Just watch that he doesn't break your heart,' said Ivy.

'Nothing like that is going to happen,' Mari insisted. 'I'm working with Huntly and that's all.'

'You'd better skedaddle,' Ivy said to Mari, checking the time. 'It's nearly eleven.'

'I'll walk up to the theatre with you,' Heather offered. 'I'm fitting Andy and some of the other actors for their costumes.'

Thanking everyone for the special celebration, Mari ran up to her flat, threw on her denim jacket, and grabbed her bags. One had her laptop. The other was a handy zipped holdall for carrying her knitting with her. She'd packed it ready to run, with two jumpers she was working on and a scarf.

Running back down, she waved through the shop window to Ivy and the others, and then walked up to the theatre, chatting to Heather.

'I see you've brought your knitting with you,' Heather remarked.

'I'm planning to knit while I'm there.'

Heather opened her bag to show what she'd purchased in the craft shop while waiting for Mari. 'I bought one of Ivy's kits to knit a black cat.' It consisted of the pattern, a picture of the finished cat, soft stuffing, and enough yarn to knit the item.

'Seeing them in the window, it's put me in the notion to knit a black cat,' Mari admitted. 'I have a pattern for a white cat I designed years ago. I could knit it in black instead.'

'You should knit it. There's always time to relax between the busy bits at the rehearsals. But this new play has certainly got everyone extra busy to get the show ready on time. I'm reworking some of the costumes.'

'I had a peek at the costumes hanging on the rails. Some of the dresses looked gorgeous. Did you make them?'

'I made a few, but I have a couple of dressmakers to help me. Drop by wardrobe and try on any of the dresses you want. I picture you'd look like a fairytale princess in one of the ball gowns.'

'I saw one that looked like it was sprinkled with starlight.'

'Those sequins and beads were added by hand. But I love making the dresses. Huntly and Niall inherited lots of the costumes when they took on the theatre, and they've bought more.'

Chatting about the costumes and knitting, they headed into the theatre around eleven.

'I'm through in wardrobe. Drop by for a chat and a cuppa.'

'I will,' said Mari.

They walked into the auditorium that was busy with activity. Huntly and Niall were down at the front seats deep in conversation, while Jon was on stage with Andy.

Heather whispered to Mari as they walked down the centre aisle. 'Is that one of your jumpers Huntly is wearing?'

He'd worn the stylish Fair Isle with dark trousers.

'Yes,' Mari confirmed. 'It suits him. He's got the broad shoulders and lean waist and hips to make it look great.'

'Maybe he's trying to impress you.'

'Ssh!' Mari scolded her playfully. 'He'll hear you. The sound carries in this theatre.'

Without turning round, Huntly spoke up. 'It certainly does.'

Heather hurried away, giggling to herself.

Blushing as she walked up to join him and Niall, Mari put on a bold smile.

'I wrote the synopsis,' she said, steering the conversation away from her embarrassment.

'Ah!' Jon announced. 'Our wordsmith is here. I need to talk to Mari before you discuss the synopsis.'

'I've emailed a copy of it to you,' Mari said to Huntly, and then she was happy to scarper away while it was read, and join Jon and Andy up on the stage.

CHAPTER SEVEN

'Fluffy is looking perky,' Mari said, looking at the cat that Andy was holding. She thought the prop manager had done an excellent makeover on his fur.

'This is Tiddles.' Andy thumbed behind him. 'Fluffy is sitting snoozing in the shop window.'

'I found Tiddles in storage,' Peter called over from the side of the stage. 'Tiddles is our action double. I've wired up his tail with pipe cleaners so we can alter his attitude.'

Andy bent the cat's tail in different poses to demonstrate this. 'I think the upright tail pose suits him.'

Mari mentally gave herself a gold star for not laughing when they were being serious about this. And then something above her on the stage caught her eye. A little silver star dangling high above them.

Huntly saw her looking at it. 'It's been up there since we took over the theatre. A prop from a show probably, or a Christmas decoration that got left up there. As it's so awkward to reach, we decided to leave it up. We'll use it as part of the night sky in the new play.'

Mari gazed up at the star glittering in the stage lighting. Then she forgot about it as the conversation swung around to the play's dialogue.

Down in the seating area, Huntly and Niall were reading and discussing the synopsis she'd written, and rather than try to gauge their reaction, she gave her full attention to Jon and Andy.

Jon held a copy of the play. 'There's a realistic quality to your dialogue in this scene,' he said, pointing to it. 'Rather than sheer theatrics, it has a raw power that I think we can amp up. It lays bare the vulnerability of Oglesby, despite his amazing abilities and the sense of mystery and magic. With Andy's delivery, the audience will empathise with the character.'

'There are two lines of dialogue,' said Andy. 'Jon thinks we should add more.'

'I can increase the dialogue,' Mari told them. 'I'd deliberately cut it down for that scene in case it slowed the pace.'

'Double it up, make it deeper and richer,' Jon encouraged her. 'Use your descriptions in the scene headings. Work them into the dialogue.'

'Okay, I'll do that.' Mari headed down to where she'd left her laptop eager to write more dialogue, taking in Jon's directions.

Huntly and Niall smiled at her.

'We're going to use your synopsis,' said Huntly. 'It's just what we need.' Then he called up to Jon. 'I've sent you a copy of Mari's synopsis. We're delighted with it.'

Jon checked his messages and began reading it right away.

'I see you've brought your knitting with you,' Niall commented to her, looking at her craft bag brimming with balls of yarn and knitting needles.

'Yes, but I'm going to rewrite the dialogue,' she said.

Niall grinned. 'I like Huntly's new jumper. Any chance you'd knit one for me in different colours?'

'Certainly. There's a colour chart on my website. Take a peek and let me know the shades you like and I'll knit it for you,' she told Niall.

Niall started looking through Mari's range of colours, unsure what he'd suit.

Mari made a suggestion. 'With your blond hair and grey eyes, the wintry greys and whites would look great on you.'

'I'll have one knitted in those colours,' Niall confirmed, happy that Mari was going to knit one for him.

'Terrific synopsis,' Jon called down to them, giving them the thumbs up.

As more props arrived and were carried up on to the stage, Mari sat down out of the way of the chaos and began to write the dialogue on her laptop.

She was accustomed to writing in quieter conditions, but told herself to buck up and get on with it. After a few minutes, the chatter faded to a buzz in the background and she found herself steeped in her story again, remembering the things she'd left behind and wrote them down until she'd more than doubled the dialogue.

When she looked up from her creative bubble, a tea trolley was being wheeled in laden with tea, coffee, cakes and sandwiches.

'Help yourself,' Huntly told her, beckoning her over.

She quickly sent the new dialogue to Jon, and then went over for a cup of tea and a tomato and salad sandwich. Was it lunchtime? Still late elevenses? She didn't know and didn't check the time, smiling as she offloaded having to live by the clock while she was in the creative cocoon of the theatre with likeminded people.

Feeling fired up, she felt herself burning up every bit of energy from the snack that kept her going until...whenever the day started to slow down.

There were moments when she managed to knit a few rows of a garment she was making. But her fingers were itching to knit a black cat. She didn't have the black yarn or a pattern with her, so she knew she'd have to forgo that fun until she got home.

Heather ran through from wardrobe a couple of times during her breaks to show Mari her handiwork.

'I've cast on the stitches to knit the cat's wee body,' said Heather. 'And knitted a few rows. It knits up quick and easy. A few more rows and then I'll have to start decreasing to shape his head.'

This only made Mari want to get stuck into knitting a kitty. 'You're doing a great job with it. You really are a good knitter.'

'I've been dressmaking all my life, and I like to knit, but your class was ideal for improving my intarsia. But this wee cat, it's a fun project. I like knitting things that I can finish in a day or an evening.'

Mari popped through to wardrobe to take a peek at the clothes later on.

'These are the outfits that I'm working on for this show.' Heather was pleased to give Mari a tour. 'This rail is exclusive for Andy's outfits. Over here are the rails for some of the other main cast. I'm sorting through the dresses for the ladies today and trying to find a memorable one for our damsel when Andy's character goes to try and save her from the clutches of those shadowy men following after her.'

It interested Mari that Heather had to know every aspect of the play's story. Learning the machinations of the work that went on behind the scenes was fascinating.

Heather's sewing machine was set up beside her fabric stash.

'I buy a lot of the fabric and trims from Ivy's shop. She has a gorgeous selection and is happy to order special items in for me,' Heather explained. 'I'm popping down later to buy sequins and braid.'

There wasn't time to try on the fairytale ballgown, but Mari planned to try it on another day. But she got to feel the beautiful blue chiffon fabric that was stitched with sparkle.

Mari was holding the dress up and looking at herself in the full–length mirror when Huntly came searching for her.

'I thought you'd have disappeared down the rabbit hole in wardrobe,' he said, casting her one of those sensual grins that set her heart rate skyrocketing.

Mari hung the dress back up. 'I was just—'

'You'd look beautiful in a ballgown like that,' said Huntly. 'Maybe there will be a grand occasion to wear it and you can borrow it for the night. Until midnight,' he joked.

'Before the fairytale ends and reality reigns once again,' said Mari.

'Fairytales can come true,' he insisted. 'Isn't that right, Heather?'

'Yes, they can,' Heather agreed. 'Look what we're all up to. A few days ago, the previous show had been cancelled and none of us knew what we were going to do. Now the theatre is a hive of activity. And Mari is a busy bee along with us.'

Huntly then explained to Mari why he'd come looking for her. 'I've been updating the theatre's website. I wondered if you'd like to take a look at it, as our official wordsmith.'

Mari smiled. 'My other new title, courtesy of Jon.'

Huntly escorted Mari away to the office to check the latest updates on the website.

She peered at the computer screen and read the banner headline, the title of the show, starring Andy, and it included her name as the playwright.

'The artwork for the show's title is great,' said Mari. It depicted a starry night sky above a city of glittering lights. The mysterious shop's windows were aglow, and Oglesby and his cat were inside.

'Sammy designed it. He worked on it until late last night.' Huntly told her.

She looked surprised.

'He's our set director nowadays, but back when he started out in theatre work years ago he designed the graphics for the show posters. Then he started getting involved in painting the scenery. He's a brilliant artist. We're fortunate to have him work for us.'

'It looks magical!' she said.

'So if you approve, would you like to press the button to make the update live?' Huntly offered.

'I'd love to.' Mari was about to press the update button, when Huntly said, 'Hang on. I'll grab of photo of you doing it, for our archives.'

Taking out his phone, he then made sure he had Mari in the picture. The computer was on the desk, and she stood there poised with her finger on the button and turned to smile at Huntly as she pressed it.

Huntly clicked a picture of her, checked the image and showed it to her.

Feeling her leaning close to view it, his heart started to thunder, and he stepped back as if she didn't affect him at all.

Mari was none the wiser, and wanted to know about the theatre's archives.

'It's something Niall and I do, to keep the special moments in the theatre, so we can look back on them and see how far we've come,' he said.

'That's a lovely idea.'

'Sammy started us off,' he admitted. 'He showed us all the old photos he had from his heydays in the theatre. Real treasures. People's smiling faces from decades ago, queuing outside theatres in the snow to see a Christmas show, or candid shots of the happy times behind the scenes. Moments from the past that shouldn't be forgotten.'

Mari realised she'd only taken photos of her knitting recently, and didn't have any pictures of herself in the city or her flat. Something to remedy soon.

Huntly accessed the theatre's archives and showed her the collection on the screen. 'This is Niall and me outside the theatre the day we took it over. It's not that long ago, but so much has happened, it seems like a lifetime.'

'I'm still trying to catch my breath with what's happened to me with the play,' she confessed. 'I think it'll take a while to sink in.'

'It will,' Huntly agreed. 'But I've sent you a copy of the picture. The first one for your archives.'

Mari checked her phone and saw the photo of herself smiling as she pressed the button.

Huntly glanced wistfully at several of the pictures from his archives. 'It'll be nice to show the grandchildren one day.'

Grandchildren? Her expression gave away her thoughts.

'I know I don't look like the settling down and raising a family type, but I live in hope of having that type of life one day, when I meet the right woman to share everything with.'

Although his tone was light, it was the most insightful thing she'd heard him say, and the feelings it stirred in her lasted even after they were interrupted by Jon coming in looking for Mari.

'I thought this would be where you were hiding,' Jon said to her. 'Come on, Andy's about to read the new dialogue.'

Beckoning her through to hear it, Mari went with Jon, leaving Huntly behind in the office, and her lingering feelings trailing behind her.

Andy stood on stage, backlit by the shop that was being constructed. Every time Mari saw the shop, Sammy and his crew had built another part of it.

The lighting guy up in the control box adjusted the spotlight, helping to create the right effect for Andy's reading, and everyone's chatter fell to a polite hush as he performed.

Mari and Jon sat in the front row and took in the new dialogue.

'Excellent, Andy,' Jon called up to him. 'I think we should do the same with the next part of the scene.' Jon turned round to look hopeful at Mari.

'I'll do that,' she said, opening up her laptop and getting ready to enrich the dialogue. Having heard the difference it made to Andy's performance, she was keen to do the same with the next paragraph.

The white–haired and bearded Sammy walked across the stage, hoisting a lightweight, old–fashioned lamp post on his shoulders. He waved to Mari as he went by.

Mari waved up to him, thinking that maybe it wouldn't take as long as she thought to feel part of this fantastical world. Then she continued typing, hearing the words in her imagination, as the laughter and chatter in the theatre faded into the background.

Mari was a fast knitter, and a fast writer. The latter came in useful for the rewrites, and she'd always had thoughts like quicksilver when writing her plays.

Jon read the new dialogue as soon as she'd written it. He approved it, and then Andy read the new material, while Sammy stealthily set up the lamp post outside the shop.

Huntly came to join Mari and Jon for the reading, and the three of them applauded as Andy finished.

Jon then directed the rehearsal for the next part of the scene that included some of the other actors.

Mari and Huntly sat in the front row of the audience seats.

Huntly stretched his long legs out in front of him and relaxed back. 'Wil is coming along to rehearse his dance show tomorrow afternoon. I promised him the use of the theatre when we hadn't anything special on, but I don't want to break my word to him and the dancers he's bringing with him. So, you'll meet Wil then if you're free.

'I'm teaching an extra knitting class at the craft shop tomorrow afternoon,' she said, wishing she could've met Wil.

'That's fine,' he assured her. 'You'll meet him another time. And eh...I wanted to ask if you'd be free to have dinner with me tomorrow night. To discuss the play, things like that.'

'Yes, I don't have any special plans for dinner.'

'Shall we say seven o'clock?' he suggested.

Mari nodded, forcing herself not to read anything extra into his invitation.

Laughter erupted on stage, involving Andy trying to create a dramatic scene with the cat as part of the props. He was using Fluffy, his personal favourite. Nothing went according to plan, and the mechanism the prop manager had stuffed inside the cat had gone awry.

'I'll read those lines again,' Andy announced as everyone burst into giggles.

'Heather showed me the cat she's knitting,' Huntly said to Mari as the chaos continued on stage. 'Andy has claimed first dibs on it when she's finished it. As a souvenir from the play. And Niall wondered if we should consider something like this for the show's merchandise. Our audiences love to buy items from our little shop in the foyer.'

'I didn't notice you had a shop,' she said. 'But I've purchased souvenirs from shows I've seen, like a mug or a tote bag.'

'We set up the shop near the box office when a show is on,' Huntly explained. 'You said you designed your own knitting patterns. Could you design a black cat for us?'

'I have a pattern for a white cat I designed years ago that I could adapt and knit in black with white whiskers and green eyes.'

'That sounds ideal,' he said.

'I'll get my class to try the new pattern tomorrow afternoon. I could work on it during the morning, and then ask if they'd like to give the pattern a go. Ivy has plenty of black yarn in stock.'

'I'll pay for any yarn or other stuff your members use,' he insisted.

Agreeing on their plan, Huntly then had to take a business call in his office.

Mari checked the files on her laptop to find the pattern for the white cat she'd designed, found it, and thought how she'd adapt it. Swapping the white yarn for black was easy. So too was using white for the whiskers and a vivid green to stitch the eyes on. The entire pattern was knitted and hand stitched with yarn, and stuffed with soft toy filling.

This could work, she thought to herself, picturing how she'd love to knit it.

Closing her laptop, she went through to wardrobe to chat to Heather.

Finding Heather within the rails of costumes, she explained about knitting a new black cat.

Heather showed her the progress she'd made on her pattern. 'It's a cute pattern, but I'd be interested in seeing your design too.'

'I'm going to show the class tomorrow,' Mari explained. 'I'll help them with whatever they're working on, but maybe a few of them would like to try knitting a black cat.'

'I'll certainly knit your design,' said Heather. 'Andy wants this cat, so I'll finish it for him. And buy more black yarn tomorrow from Ivy's shop.'

'Huntly is paying for the yarn and the soft filling anyone in the class uses,' said Mari.

'That's kind of him. It should be a fun class. My hours are flexible, so I'll be there in the afternoon after working in the theatre all morning.'

Mari glanced around to check that no one was eavesdropping on their conversation. 'Huntly has invited me to have dinner with him tomorrow evening upstairs in his turret,' Mari whispered.

'Oooh! How romantic.'

'Ssh! You know how voices carry here.'

Heather giggled and kept her voice to a whisper. 'Is Huntly going to cook dinner? He's a marvellous cook. Not that he's made dinner for me, but he's baked cakes for us before and they were delicious.'

'Yes, he's cooking dinner. I've no idea what he's planning to make.'

'Romantic overtures will surely be on the menu.'

Mari tried not to smile. 'No, nothing like that will happen. We're working on the play.'

Heather gave her a knowing look and a grin. 'Huntly is sooo handsome though.'

'Stop it, you're making me blush.'

'And I still think he's quite taken with you.'

'I've no plans to have my heart broken,' Mari insisted, forgetting to keep her voice down.

Huntly, having finished his business call, had come looking for Mari, and overheard her comment.

Heather gestured to a rail of dresses, and tried to stifle her giggles. 'These are some of the costumes I'm reworking for the show,' she prattled to Mari.

'They're gorgeous dresses,' said Mari, brushing aside her previous remark. 'Such lovely fabric.'

'I wanted to talk to you about the production,' Huntly said to Mari. 'Jon's suggesting an idea for one of the scenes and I'd like your thoughts on it too.'

Mari smiled and walked away with Huntly, wondering if he'd say anything about her remark.

As they headed to the stage he glanced at her. 'Is there someone you're concerned will break your heart?'

Mari stomach flipped. 'It was just silly gossip we were chatting about,' she lied, hearing the tension in her voice.

Huntly pressed his firm lips together and nodded as they continued walking along.

But Mari sensed he suspected she'd been talking about him.

'Are we still on for dinner tomorrow night?' he said.

'Yes,' Mari replied brightly. 'I'm looking forward to it, and to seeing the view of Edinburgh from your world.'

CHAPTER EIGHT

Huntly stood beside the classic baby grand piano, taking a phone call, deep in conversation, as Mari got ready to leave the theatre for the night. He was reflected in the high gloss black finish of the beautiful piano.

It was early evening, or so she gauged, and a lot of the activity was starting to wane, so she decided to head home. Glancing over at Huntly, she picked up her bags.

Unaware she was leaving, he didn't see her walk away.

Jon had a prior dinner engagement and had just left, and Andy had gone home to relax and learn his dialogue. Niall was still buzzing around the theatre and was currently backstage.

As Mari stepped outside the theatre into the sepia glow of the evening, she breathed deeply and looked up at the sky. An amber glow of the approaching golden hour arched over the cobbled street, making everything look like it was a throwback to a vintage era.

The classic architecture, the cobbles, and the eclectic mix of eateries had a traditional quality, and she felt herself unwind as she walked home to her flat.

The chatter and sounds floating out from the nightlife, drifted to a soft buzz in the background as she went over the highlights of her day. Particularly those moments with Huntly, the man she now had a dinner date with, though not a date in the romantic sense, which eased the pressure of putting her heart in jeopardy.

Approaching the craft shop, she saw that it was closed, but smiled to herself when she saw all the little black cats, knitted, crocheted or sewn, sitting in the window display.

Heading through the close, she went up to her flat and closed the door on a memorable day.

The sepia glow outside her windows cast autumn shadows through the flat, and she turned a couple of lamps on and flicked the lights on in the kitchen.

She unpacked her knitting bag and set up her laptop on her desk while deciding what to have for dinner.

Opting for a bowl of hearty lentil soup, she heated that up and served it with salad and bread.

Sitting in the kitchen, she ate her dinner, then washed the dishes and went through to the living room sipping a mug of tea.

The first thing she wanted to do was work on the black cat pattern. Searching through her stash of yarn, she picked out a ball of black double knit, and the other colours she needed. Then she used the same size of knitting needles to cast on the required stitches that she'd designed for the white cat.

Taking a note of anything she adapted in the pattern, she upgraded it slightly, improving the pattern to make the black cat design even better. Keeping the pattern easy for others to knit, she used garter stitch, and the rows knitted up quickly. Increasing and decreasing the stitches where needed to create the shape for the cat, she sat by the window, glancing at the darkening sky.

Having knitted the pieces she needed, she stitched them together with yarn, and then stuffed the cat with a few handfuls of soft toy filling. Then she added the white whiskers, pink nose and green eyes, all stitched on using yarn.

She'd just finished making the cat when she saw a light shining from inside the old shop across the street.

There was a light on! Thinking this was her chance to peek in the window and perhaps see the elusive owner, she put her pumps on and ran downstairs.

By the time she emerged from the close, she saw the light turn off in the shop window, but she ran across anyway and peered in. But there was nothing except the usual shapes and shadows.

Glancing up and down the street, she didn't see any sign of the owner, but there was Spindle, sitting in front of the craft shop.

Mari smiled. The real cat looked like he was part of the display of stuffed cats.

'Hello, Spindle,' she called over to him. She was sure he reacted to the name.

Remembering what Huntly had said about taking photos of special moments, she dug her phone out from the pocket of her cords and went to take a picture of the cat sitting in front of the shop.

Then she had a better idea, and turned around, held the phone at arm's length, so she could capture herself in the picture with Spindle and the craft shop in the background.

Her finger was poised on the button, but the second she went to press it, a bolt of lightning flashed across the night sky, causing her to jump as she pressed it.

When she checked the image, she'd inadvertently tilted the phone back, and she had a wonderful photo of the lightning in the sky, a glimpse of herself looking startled and the stuffed cats in the background. But no sign of Spindle. The cat had run off, disappearing into the shadows of a dark close.

Shivering as a low rumble of thunder indicated that a storm was on its way, she hurried back up to her flat and put the kettle on for a cup of tea.

While it boiled, she added the picture to a file on her laptop she named, archives, along with a copy of the one Huntly had taken of her in the theatre office. It was only two pictures, but it was a start.

Making her tea, she then took several photos of the flat, the cosy living room, the bedroom and kitchen, and the views from the windows. More memories for her archives.

As she finished adding the photos, a call came through from Huntly.

His face peered out the phone at her. 'I didn't get a chance to thank you before you left the theatre this evening. You've been a great help with getting the production up and running.'

'I'm enjoying being part of it,' she said. 'You were busy on a call when I was about to leave. I didn't want to interrupt.'

'Word is getting around that we're putting on the new play. People are calling, interested in being involved, or wanting to know if they can come to the opening night.'

'It's exciting.'

'It is.' Seeing her smile at him, he wanted to talk to her about having no intention of breaking her heart, but unlike her, he couldn't find the right words. Instead, a tense silence lingered for a moment.

Mari sensed the tension and decided to tell him about the new pattern. 'I've knitted a black cat from a pattern I'd designed, changing the colours of the yarn.'

'That was fast work.'

'It's an easy pattern, and I've knitted it in white before, and I've made lots of other soft toys.'

She held up the knitted cat and showed it to him.

Huntly smiled when he saw it. 'It's perfect.'

'I'll tidy up the notes I've made for the pattern, and then use this as a project for the knitting class tomorrow afternoon. If there are any bits of the pattern that they find are too fiddly or need improved, I'll make the alterations. Then I'll send you a copy of the finished pattern for you to read through.'

'Thank you, Mari.'

'And I've started to take pictures for my own archives.' She told him what happened earlier.

'You saw a light on inside the old shop?' Huntly sounded interested.

'Yes, but by the time I ran down to have a look in the window, it turned off and the shop was in darkness again.'

'Did you see anyone leave?'

'No, but I did see Spindle.' She explained about the flash of lightning frightening the cat and it running away.

'I heard the thunder when I was in the theatre.' He was still there, standing up on the stage.

Mari peered out the living room window and showed him the view she had. 'The storm seems to have blown by. All bluff and thunder.'

He felt like that talking to her. There were things he wanted to say, and yet he knew he shouldn't as it could only lead to trouble, including broken hearts for both of them.

'I love thunderstorms,' she said. 'As long as I'm cosy indoors, and able to watch the drama from my window. Or tucked up in bed listening to the rain battering down.'

'Snuggled up safe and sound.'

Mari nodded and smiled out at him, causing his heart to ache with a longing he blamed on being overtired.

'It's been a long day,' he said, easing the tension from his shoulders. 'I'll let you get some rest.'

She peered behind him. He seemed to be the only one left on the stage. 'Are you finished at the theatre now too?'

'I wish,' said Huntly. He still had phone calls to make. People wanted to discuss the new show. And maybe he'd imagined it, but he thought he saw something twinkle above him as he said this. He blinked, but couldn't see what it was.

'Goodnight,' she said, finishing the call. 'I'll see you tomorrow night.'

And with a smile, she was gone.

He put his phone in his pocket and sighed, and wished he could let true love and romance into his busy life.

And there it was again, a glimmer of silver sparkle in the shaded light of the stage. Gazing up, there was nothing except shadows.

Shrugging to himself, he walked off the stage, turned all the lights off in the theatre, and headed through to the office to finish making those calls.

After typing the changes she'd made to the cat pattern, she sent a copy to Ivy so that she could print it out for any class members wanting to participate in knitting it.

Then she noticed the other plays she'd written on her laptop, and started to read through one of them, seeing it with a fresh eye, one that felt more confident that her play had potential. An earlier work, she'd always loved the story.

Time wisped by as it tended to do when she became engrossed in her playwriting, and when she finally glanced up, she realised she needed to get to bed.

Snuggled under the covers, she planned how she'd organise her busy day ahead. She thought about popping out early for fresh groceries, having breakfast and then catching up on her knitting, taking the class and trying out the new black cat pattern...and fell asleep before she thought about having dinner with Huntly.

The golden sunshine emphasised the burnished colours of the bright autumn morning as Mari headed back to her flat with a bag of fresh groceries.

Dressed in a vintage, deep marigold shirt, dark green cords and pumps, she'd teamed it with one of her own knitted vests, like a sleeveless jumper, in autumnal shades from russet and gingerbread to bronze and butterscotch.

These vests were popular with her customers. They knitted up quick, some were plain coloured, but most were patterned, like the one she was wearing. The latter were great for adding colour and style to a plain shirt. The vests and waistcoats she knitted provided a cosy layer of comfy warmth.

Mari had just finished unpacking her groceries in the kitchen when a message came through on her website. Thinking it was a customer order, she checked it, and was taken aback when she saw it was from the last person she imagined she'd hear from — Scarlet.

She'd used the website to send Mari a message:

Will you meet me for coffee this morning? Scarlet named one of the cafes nearby. *I'd like to chat to you about your playwriting. And make amends for squabbling.*

Mari was surprised and intrigued. She checked the time. Instead of making breakfast, she decided to take Scarlet up on her offer. The cafe served delicious breakfasts, and she wanted to hear what Scarlet had to say.

They arrived outside the cafe at the same time. Scarlet wore a fashionable red skirt suit that matched her name in vibrancy.

'Thanks for agreeing to meet me,' Scarlet said as Mari walked up to her.

They went inside the stylish cafe and took a window seat. Scarlet perused the menu. 'I haven't had breakfast.'

'Neither have I.'

'Let's have breakfast then, my treat,' Scarlet insisted.

'Do you want to share a breakfast platter? I love the croissants they serve here. But it's always too much for one.'

Scarlet brightened. 'Oh, yes.' She studied the menu. 'It includes fresh fruit, yogurt and whipped cream.'

'And strawberry and raspberry jam.'

A mischievous smiled passed between them.

Scarlet ordered the shared breakfast. It was served up quickly, allowing them to sit in the shaded sunlight and enjoy the delicious fruits, from blueberries to raspberries, and melon and grapes, with yogurt and cream. And a pot of tea for two.

They both helped themselves to the pastries first, filling them with strawberry jam and cream, smiling that they had something in common.

'This will keep me going until—' Mari almost let slip that she was having dinner with Huntly. The mood between them was light, and Mari didn't want to spoil it.

'Until you're at the theatre later tonight,' Scarlet finished for her.

Mari nodded and bit into her croissant.

'We shouldn't squabble over Huntly,' Scarlet stated.

Mari glanced over at her, gauging whether Scarlet was a potential friend or foe. No decision made, she kept to the neutral zone and feigned more interest in her breakfast than in Huntly.

'Or maybe Niall is more your type.'

The look in Mari's eyes settled that suggestion.

'No, Niall's nice, but he's not my type either,' said Scarlet.

Mari poured their tea. 'I don't want to become romantically involved with anyone at the moment. I have a chance to build my career as a playwright.'

'What you want, and what the real world will throw at you are totally different.'

Mari sipped her tea.

Scarlet poured milk into her tea and stirred it. 'Huntly and Niall are both catches. It's an unfortunate fact. Rich, handsome, actually nice, except when Huntly is in his blunt mode, which is fairly often. Though I think it's because he doesn't have any real love in his life, so he gets grumpy and uses that as a front to shield himself.' She shrugged. 'But what do I know? Maybe he's just a grouch.'

'They own a theatre. I'm still knitting.'

'I act. You write plays. We belong in their world.'

'For work, yes, but it doesn't mean we have to fall for them,' said Mari.

'They're both luscious, so of course we're going to twist ourselves into knots whenever we're within kissing distance of them.'

Mari laughed.

Scarlet sighed. 'And don't even get me started on Jon.'

Mari's interest sparked. 'You like Jon?'

Scarlet looked at her across the table, and those icy eyes of hers showed a hint of warmth.

The penny dropped. 'But Huntly and the others think—'

Scarlet took a sip of her tea, and gave Mari a knowing look.

'Does Jon know how you feel about him?' There was an urgency to Mari's tone.

'No. But none of them can see past Huntly, and Huntly can't see past himself.'

Mari leaned back in her chair while Scarlet ate a spoonful of blueberries and yogurt. 'Wow! That changes the battle lines.'

'I don't want to squabble with you, Mari. I thought maybe we could team up, or at least share gossip.'

'I've no gossip to tell. Nothing of note anyway.'

Scarlet wrapped her fingers around her cup, displaying her manicured red nails. 'But I have. That's what I wanted to talk to you about.'

CHAPTER NINE

'I came to Huntly and Niall's theatre because I wanted a part in the new play,' Scarlet explained to Mari. 'I loved what I'd heard about your story. But I had been offered a role in a rival production.'

'So everything you said was true.'

'Yes. But Huntly thinks I want to date him, and I don't. I've always wanted to be in his productions because they're new.' She sighed. 'I know I can be difficult to work with sometimes, but I'm trying not to be so overly dramatic.'

Mari topped up their tea. 'What did you want to talk to me about?'

'The director I'm working with has been in the theatre for years. He's a seasoned director. The show that I'm in with him is a classic, and I'm enjoying the role. But he's heard about you, Mari, a new playwright on the scene, and he's planning to contact you to discuss any other new plays you're working on.'

Mari was taken aback. 'I haven't heard from him.'

'He'll probably contact you soon, as I did, via your website. Or maybe you'll let me give him your personal contact. He's eager to read any new plays of yours that would be suitable for his schedule.'

'If he's Huntly's rival, wouldn't that be awkward?'

'Jon directs shows for other theatres. Andy and I act in various productions. You need to have the same options.'

Mari frowned. 'I haven't had time to think about that. I've only just had my first play accepted.'

'Yes, but now others will be interested in your work. And you're going to be included in media interviews for the new play. I've heard that Huntly and Niall are due to be interviewed for a magazine feature. As the playwright, you'll be expected to be part of it.'

'I don't want to be in the limelight,' said Mari. 'I'd prefer to stay in the background.'

Scarlet repeated her comment from earlier. 'What you want, and what the real world will throw at you are totally different.'

Mari's thoughts were cast into turmoil. 'I didn't think I'd be interviewed.'

'It's part of the business. But you're a confident young woman. You can handle chatting about your work,' Scarlet said, bolstering her.

Mari took a calming breath, sensing Scarlet was right.

'Look what you've achieved on your own,' Scarlet added.

'Is this the gossip you wanted to tell me?'

'Yes, and to say that if you talk to my director, I'm interested in any leading parts in the plays. Let's keep in touch.'

'Okay,' said Mari. 'I'm planning to work on my other plays.'

Scarlet added a final comment. 'And everything I've said, you don't need to keep it a secret. You're welcome to tell Huntly or others. It's all going to be the latest gossip soon.'

Mari nodded, relieved that she didn't need to keep it to herself, and then they continued to eat their breakfast.

Scarlet frowned and studied Mari's vest. 'What is that you're wearing? Did you knit it yourself?'

'It's one of my vests. I create my own patterns.'

'I love the autumn colours.'

'The vests are handy for layering. On autumn days like this when it's not too cold I like to wear one instead of a jacket.'

'I'd like one. It would be quite fashionable in a classic, vintage sort of way. And I'd benefit from the brighter colours.' Scarlet's lips formed into a smirk.

Mari smiled back at her. 'You're scarlet bright this morning.'

'I didn't want another scolding for being dull.'

And then they laughed and continued chatting and enjoying their breakfast.

Later, Mari and Scarlet walked out into the morning sunlight, still chatting and then they went their separate ways, promising to speak soon.

Back at her flat, Mari got on with her busy day, fired up on the delicious breakfast and gossip.

She smiled to herself when she saw that one of the vests had been purchased from her website. Seeing it was for Scarlet, Mari packed it up ready for posting.

Working through lunchtime, she got some knitting done, sitting by the window, looking out at the view and thinking about her plays. She had a lot of things to juggle in her schedule now that she was involved in the theatre, but making dreams come true required hard work. And flexibility. She hadn't planned to teach the class how to knit a cat, but...

Ivy's craft shop was set up for the knitting class when Mari went down, carrying her parcel orders, in the early afternoon.

'I've printed out several copies of the black cat pattern,' Ivy said, sounding enthusiastic. 'And I have plenty of black yarn and the other colours ready. I'm sure most of the members will want to have a go at knitting it.' Ivy dug out the half–finished one she was working on. 'I couldn't resist. The pattern is easy. No changes that I'd make. It knits up well with this yarn.'

Mari had brought the one she'd made to show to the class, took it out of her bag, and sat it on one of the tables. 'I enjoyed knitting mine.'

'Oh, he's lovely,' said Ivy.

They were talking about the pattern when Heather arrived.

'I'm a wee bit early for the class,' Heather said to them. 'But I wanted to buy more spools of the light grey thread to take back with me later to the theatre. It blends in so well with everything when I'm sewing the costumes.'

Ivy knew the thread Heather wanted and went to bag it for her.

'Can I have a word with you before the class starts?' Mari said in an urgent whisper to Heather.

'Yes, is something wrong?'

'I'm busy rustling around,' Ivy said, thinking they needed privacy.

'It's okay, Ivy,' Mari assured her. 'I had breakfast with Scarlet this morning, and she had a lot to tell me.'

Heather and Ivy listened as Mari relayed the details of how her morning had unfolded.

Heather stared wide–eyed at Mari. 'Scarlet fancies Jon! Not Huntly.'

Mari nodded. 'It changes everything. Huntly doesn't need to side–step Scarlet thinking she wants to be his girlfriend. She wanted to be in the new play, but it's Jon she likes.'

Ivy was doing her best to keep up. 'Jon's the director, isn't he?'

'He is,' said Heather. 'We all thought Scarlet fancied Huntly.' Then she thought about this. 'Mind you, I only heard about that from gossip. I wonder what Jon would do if he knew that Scarlet was interested in him?'

'Is the director handsome?' Ivy said to them.

'Jon is suave and a good looking man,' said Mari.

'Oooh! What a romantic pickle.' Ivy giggled, but then a few of the class members came in, all smiles and chatter.

'I thought you should know what Scarlet told me,' Mari whispered to Heather, and then she started to welcome the members and organise the class.

All the members wanted to knit a black cat.

Ivy set up paper bags and popped the necessary yarn into each one along with a copy of the pattern.

Mari handed them out to the members. 'The theatre is paying for the yarn and the stuffing.' A large bag of soft stuffing was available for them to help themselves. Spare sets of knitting needles were on hand, but most of them had the required size of needles.

Eager to get started, the members began knitting the pattern. From beginners to experienced knitters like Heather, they agreed that they found the pattern easy and fun to make.

While tea and cakes were served during the class, Heather whispered to Mari. 'Are you going to tell Huntly what Scarlet said?'

'Yes, I think he should know,' Mari confided to her.

'During the last show that Scarlet was part of at the theatre, she was often arguing with Jon,' said Heather. 'But she was usually just trying to improve her lines, or whatever else it was.'

Ivy came over and handed one of the paper bags to Mari. 'I've filled this bag with the yarn, the pattern for the cat, and stuffing, so you can take it with you to show Huntly how the kit would look.'

'That's so handy,' said Mari. 'I'll give this to him tonight.'

The class continued until the late afternoon, and then the members left, taking their knitted cats with them.

After helping Ivy to tidy up the shop, Mari went up to her flat to get ready for dinner with Huntly.

Huntly popped out to buy extra groceries for the dinner he planned to cook. His bag was filled with tomatoes, red, orange and yellow peppers, lettuce, greentails, and a fresh loaf of bread.

He walked past the craft shop on his way back to the theatre. The fading amber sunlight glinted off the front window and the pretty bunting fluttered in the light breeze, but the shop was closed. He smiled to himself when he saw the array of little knitted and crafted cats on display.

Looking up at Mari's window, he felt the urge to drop by and see her. During his hectic day, she'd regularly drifted through his thoughts. But he continued walking up the street, enjoying the atmosphere of the city as the day unwound. There was no chance that he could do likewise, not with everything he had to do.

Mari put on a sky blue jumper, a wrap skirt in a soft dark blue jersey fabric, and a pair of court shoes.

Tucking the sample kit in her bag, she headed out into the calm evening and walked up the street to the theatre, wondering how the night would unfold.

She arrived at quarter to seven, picturing that Huntly would welcome her and show her up to the turret for dinner.

But nothing went according to plan.

'Mari!' Huntly waved to her from the stage as she walked in. He wore a white shirt, dark trousers and a bronze and gold brocade waistcoat.

A man, similar in age and height to Huntly, with dark hair and a fit build, wearing a classic black suit, was leaping about the stage, dancing to dramatic music.

Mari recognised the well–known dancer.

'Come and meet Wil,' Huntly said to her.

Mari was introduced to Wil.

'Huntly tells me you're from the coastal town where I've opened up my new dance studio.' Wil's blue eyes were bright with enthusiasm, pleased to meet her.

'Yes, I heard about your new studio, but I've since moved here to the city,' said Mari. 'I saw you perform last year in Edinburgh. You're a wonderful dancer. I enjoyed the show.'

'Thank you, Mari,' said Wil. 'Huntly's been telling me all about the new play you've written. It sounds great. I'll be coming along to see it one evening.' Wil gestured to the stage. 'I'm rehearsing choreography for my new show.'

Professional dance couples were practising to the music. The men were suited and the ladies wore ballgowns. And Sammy had created a starry night sky setting using the lighting effect from the play.

Mari felt the excitement all around her.

'Do you dance?' Wil called to her.

Mari shook her head. 'No, I'm not a dancer, but I do enjoy watching others perform.'

'Put a ballgown on and come up and waltz around,' said Wil. 'We're going to take pictures for a joint promotion. Find a dress in wardrobe and come and dance with me.'

Heather beckoned Mari to hurry away with her to wardrobe.

Not wanting to put a dampener on the offer to dance with someone like Wil, Mari let herself be swept into the whirlwind of excitement and mayhem backstage.

'What's going on?' Mari said to Heather as they hurried along.

'Huntly and Niall have a journalist friend. He was going to interview them for a magazine feature about the new play.'

'Scarlet mentioned this,' Mari confirmed.

'Well, Wil and his dancers were scheduled to come along today and use the stage for a dress rehearsal for their new dance show. But then Huntly suggested to the journalist that Wil be included in the interview, to make a real splash of publicity for both of them. And the journalist is eager to do this. He thinks it'll be a great feature for the magazine.'

'Do I need to talk to the journalist?'

'Yes, and have your photo taken, so let's get you ready for the ball.'

Niall ran by them. He wore a classic suit, shirt and tie. 'Bring Mari up to speed on what we're doing please, Heather.'

'I'm getting her dressed,' Heather called after him.

A lovely young woman around the same age as Mari was heading in the same direction as Niall.

'Mari, this is Delphie,' Heather said, introducing her briefly. 'She's going to be waltzing with Wil and Niall.'

'Pleased to meet you, Mari,' said Delphie.

Delphine, known as Delphie, hurried on. Her chestnut hair was pinned up in a chignon and she wore a gorgeous fairytale ballgown.

Other dancers were running around getting ready, and there was such a feeling of excitement in the air that Mari decided to put on the sparkling blue ballgown she'd seen recently and join in the photo shoot. More memories for the archives.

Heather helped Mari on with her dress. 'You look a treat,' said Heather.

Mari smiled and admired the dress in the mirror, seeing the chiffon sparkle under the lights. 'It's beautiful, but I can't dance.'

Huntly's voice spoke over her shoulder. 'I'm sure you can manage a waltz, especially in a dress like that. It was made for dancing under the stars.'

Clasping Mari's hand, Huntly led her away, on to the stage, where Wil took charge of her.

An experienced dancer and choreographer, Wil took Mari in hold, instructing her and encouraging her as the music began. The stage lighting made her dress sparkle like starlight.

Mari found herself being swept across the stage in Wil's capable arms, waltzing as best she could, thankful that the long dress disguised any mistakes she made.

'Just dance,' Wil said to her. 'I'll keep you right.'

And he did. Mari couldn't stop smiling as she was whirled around the floor by Wil, her feet barely touching the floor as his strength lifted her.

Peter and Sammy were recording this and taking photos with their phones. Jon and Andy were there joining in the fun.

As the music changed, Huntly stepped in and began dancing with Mari, and Wil then waltzed with Delphie. Other dance couples were circling around, creating a wonderful scene.

And there was Mari, in the heart of it, waltzing with Huntly under a theatrical starry sky.

'Dinner will be a little later than planned,' Huntly said to Mari as they continued dancing. The music had changed again, this time to a slow waltz, and she felt his arms gently pull her closer to him.

Gazing up at him, she smiled. 'Your world is full of surprises.'

'Our world, Mari. This is your world now too.'

As the slow waltz finished with a flourish, Huntly dipped Mari, and she played along, letting his strong arms hold her as she leaned back. His face was a breath away from hers.

For one crazy moment, Huntly almost gave in to the temptation to kiss her, but he knew this would ruin the playful mood.

Instead, Huntly clasped her around the waist and helped her stand up. He still towered over her and they were standing within kissing distance.

Aware they were being photographed by Peter and Sammy, they stepped back from each other, smiling.

The journalist waved them over for the interview, along with Niall, Jon and Andy.

Mari was taken aback that the journalist wanted to know about her playwriting before throwing questions to the others.

'Yes, this is my first play that's been accepted for production,' Mari confirmed.

'What are you writing now?' the journalist prompted her, hoping for a snippet of exciting things to come.

'I'm reworking two plays I wrote before The Shop That Sells Everything,' said Mari. 'And this morning, while I was sitting knitting and gazing out the window at one of my favourite views of Edinburgh, my mind was sparking with fresh ideas that I'm eager to start writing.'

'Huntly mentioned that you're from a small, coastal town not too far from here,' said the journalist. He seemed interest to hear about her writing process. 'Do you find that Edinburgh inspires your playwriting?'

'I do,' Mari told him. 'And since I've met Huntly, his tendency to attract drama has added to my ideas for new plays.'

Mari's light–hearted remark went down well, and Huntly gave an exaggerated bow.

'How did you first meet Huntly?' The journalist was recording every word of her comments.

Mari glanced at Huntly and then gave a brief reply. 'He'd been slaying dragons in the theatre all day, and ran after me dressed in fencing gear, with a prop sword, causing a furore.'

'True, all true,' Huntly said, grinning.

Details were added for further interest, then Niall, Jon and Andy were interviewed.

Listening to them, Mari thought that this would make an interesting feature. And even more so when Wil's comments about rehearsing his new dance show at the theatre were added to it.

'I'll get this feature written up quickly,' said the journalist, switching off his phone and getting ready to leave. 'It'll be in the next issue of the magazine, which is out soon, but it'll be up on our online issue by tomorrow night along with lots of pics and video clips. I'll keep you posted.'

'Thanks, we're looking forward to it,' said Huntly, walking him out. Niall, Jon and Andy went with them.

Mari stood watching them go, and then looked up at Wil and his dancers, and Delphie, packing up everything they'd brought with them and getting ready to leave too.

The music was switched off and the lights were dimmed, and the theatre crew headed home.

They all seemed so accustomed to packing up their world of make believe, that Mari found herself almost alone in front of the stage, watching them disappear into the night.

Wil and the others had a drive home ahead of them, but there was a sense of everyone winding down.

But Mari's evening was just gearing up as Huntly came striding back in, all smiles and energy.

'Shall we?' he said, gesturing to her to come with him.

'I'll just change out of this ballgown,' said Mari. 'I'll be right back.'

As she turned to hurry away, Huntly clasped hold of her hand. 'It's not midnight yet, Cinderella. Let's have dinner.'

Mari smiled. 'I can't wear a fairytale dress for our dinner.'

Huntly kept hold of her hand. 'Dinner in a turret with a magical view of the city. I think it's the perfect dress.'

Laughing, she let Huntly lead her to the stairs.

'Let's take the scenic route,' he said.

One set of stairs provided access to the turret from inside the theatre. The other set was outside.

Huntly opened the door to the outside route that had a sensational view.

'It's a beautiful evening,' said Huntly. He hadn't let go of her hand, and gave it a reassuring squeeze.

Mari surprised herself by stepping outside, feeling the autumn air waft through the chiffon of her ballgown as Huntly led her up towards the turret.

'Wait,' she said suddenly, causing him to jolt and pause. 'I want to see the view of the city.'

Huntly smiled, and for a few moments they stood there together gazing at the view of Edinburgh at night, lights sparkling all around them.

This wasn't just a memory for the archives she thought, this was something she'd never forget. Maybe this was the most special moment she'd ever share with Huntly. Or maybe this was the start of more excitement and drama with him.

CHAPTER TEN

Mari stood in Huntly's living room gazing out the windows. 'This is an incredible view.' The lights of the city were sparkling all around and the inky sky was filled with stars.

Nightglow shone through the windows, illuminating the living room. He'd kept the lights off for a few minutes so she could see the view.

'All the rooms in the turret have a great view,' said Huntly, gesturing to his bedroom, a spare room and the kitchen.

Her ballgown shimmered as she walked around, taking in the views from the kitchen after peering into Huntly's bedrooms from the hallway, and avoiding any awkwardness of overstepping his privacy.

The entire apartment was stylishly furnished in light neutral tones, predominantly beige, white and light grey. It had exclusive quality to it, but he made her welcome.

'Feel free to wander around. I'll rustle us up dinner.' He turned the lights on in the kitchen. Spotlights illuminated key features, like the work surface where he started to prepare the tomatoes, peppers and salad vegetables. Rows of twinkle lights edged their way around parts of the cupboards and the classic dresser, creating a theatre–like atmosphere amid the high level of cooking equipment.

Shiny pots and pans hung from one of the walls. They looked like they were used rather than a token gesture, but shone as if they'd been well–cleaned and properly stored. That was the feeling Mari had as she glanced around the kitchen from the doorway. If she hadn't known better, she would've assumed Huntly was a top chef.

Seeing the efficient methods he used to rustle up their dinner, she didn't offer to assist him, as she was sure she'd be a hindrance. Wearing a fairytale ballgown, she certainly wasn't dressed to be his assistant.

Mari lingered in the doorway watching him chip–chop the orange, red and yellow peppers.

'Come in and take a seat.' Huntly motioned to one of the chairs around the kitchen table.

She drifted in a wisp of sparkling blue chiffon and sat down. The dining table in the living was set for an intimate dinner for two. This table had a salad bowl that Huntly was topping up with the peppers and tomatoes.

Glancing at the stove, nothing appeared to be cooking on the hobs, but the delicious aroma of a savoury dish filled the air.

'The pie is in the oven,' he said. 'I prepared it earlier so I could just heat it up.'

'It smells delicious.' She hadn't realised how hungry she was, having had nothing substantial since breakfast at the cafe.

'I hope you're hungry. It's a savoury potato pie. I heard you talking about what you liked when we had dinner with Jon and Andy.' He described the contents, chunks of potato, chopped onion, greentails, Scottish cheddar cheese and seasoning. He'd even made his own shortcrust pastry.

When he opened the oven to check the pie, she saw that he'd decorated the top of the pie with shortcrust star shapes.

'I'm impressed,' Mari told him.

'I love to cook.' Huntly looked like he was in his element, moving around the kitchen with practised ease.

He'd clearly made an effort and yet it wasn't an exertion for him to rustle up their dinner. Soon, she was being shooed through to the living room where he started to serve up dinner for two.

She sat down at the table he'd set with classic white plates, silverware, linen napkins and glass table lamps that flickered with candlelight. Lamps in the living room added to the warm glow, but didn't eclipse the view of the glittering lights outside the windows.

Serving up two generous slices of the potato pie with its golden shortcrust pastry, and a side salad sprinkled with greentails, he offered her scoops of chutney. Mari opted for bramble.

'Thank you for this,' she said, wondering when to broach on the subject of Scarlet, not wanting to break the fairytale atmosphere.

Huntly spoke up first as they tucked into their meal. 'I invited you to dinner so we could talk in private. We haven't had a chance since we met.' He sounded as if there was something specific on his mind.

Mari steeled herself. Was the fairytale about to be shattered or tainted with a dose of reality?

He took a deep breath and looked across the table at her. His heart took a hit every time he dropped his guard and let himself believe that he should ask her out on a proper date. Tonight wasn't the right time, and maybe there never would be, as he began...

'You're a talented writer. We're pushing ahead with the publicity for the play. The journalist from the magazine is only the start of it.' He took another deep breath. 'The thing is, other theatres and directors are bound to take an interest and will approach you with offers to write for them, or to snap up any new plays you've written or are currently writing.'

Mari nodded, letting him get it all out in the open.

'As you're not experienced in this industry, I thought I should discuss this with you. I've already had a couple of people I know in this business call me about this. And murmurings from others getting wind that there's a new and exciting talent in our midst.'

'Word seems to travel fast.'

'The touch paper has been lit. Now you'll have to decide what your next move is that will benefit your career. Bluntly, and I hope I'm not overstepping, but you strike me as a level–headed but career driven young woman, so I don't want you to feel awkward about accepting offers that would further your playwriting. Of course, Niall and I want first dibs on your new plays, but we wouldn't dream of holding you back. That wouldn't benefit any of us in the long run. And most of all, it wouldn't be right for you, and we've no intention of creating tensions and theatrics.'

'Phew! That's a relief, because that's one of the things I wanted to talk to you about.'

Huntly gestured for her to tell him what was on her mind while he ate his dinner.

'Scarlet says her director wants to talk to me about any new plays I'm working on.'

'Scarlet?' This certainly took him aback.

Mari explained about them having breakfast and what they'd discussed regarding her new plays. She kept the second topic under wraps for the moment.

'Has her director contacted you yet?'

'No, but he may have done by now. I've left my phone in my bag down in wardrobe. I'd brought a copy of the knitted cat pattern with me too.'

Huntly had switched his phone off, not wanting them to be disturbed while they had dinner. 'Leave it there for now. Check it later. Let's talk. What was the other thing you wanted to tell me.'

Here goes, Mari thought, unsure how he'd react to the news. 'Scarlet likes Jon.'

Huntly frowned. 'She's always arguing with him. He rubs her feathers up the wrong way.'

Mari shook her head. 'No, she acts that way because she's in love with him.'

Huntly sat back in his chair and his eyes showed his total surprise. 'So, she's not...'

'Scarlet has no wish to date you.' There was no way to sugar the pill.

'Well, that's...wonderful.'

They went on to discuss the ramifications of this reveal.

'Does she intend telling Jon?' he said.

'I rather get the impression that she'd like me to fan the flames of that gossip. She told me that none of this needs to be kept a secret.'

A mischievous expression lit up Huntly's face. 'Then let's tell Jon before he hears it secondhand from someone else.'

'I don't know Jon well enough. You should tell him.'

Huntly needed little encouragement. He switched his phone back on and made the call. 'I can't wait to see his face when he hears this,' he said quickly to Mari. 'Despite everything Jon says about Scarlet being annoying and whatever, he thinks she's gorgeous. But he's convinced she doesn't like him.'

Jon's face peered out casually at Huntly as he accepted the call.

Mari listened as Huntly told him the news, not sugaring the pill either. She could hear Jon's reaction, and Huntly turned the phone around so she could see him too.

Jon looked like he wanted to be happy about this, but was wondering if they were playing a joke on him.

'It's true. Scarlet told me,' Mari assured Jon.

'And we all thought it was heartthrob Huntly that she fancied,' said Jon, keeping a lid on his reaction.

'So...' Huntly said to him.

'So what?' Jon replied.

'It's your move, Jon.'

Jon baulked at Huntly's suggestion. 'I can't just call Scarlet up and say, hey, I hear we all had the wrong end of the stick, so do you want to go out to dinner with me?'

'Why not?' said Huntly.

Jon hesitated.

'Call her,' Mari encouraged him. 'Invite her out to dinner.'

Jon peered out at them. 'Is that a candlelight dinner you two matchmakers are having?'

'We are,' Huntly confirmed. 'But we're just talking shop and putting the world to rights.'

'Starting with me risking having my heart skewed and fried by Scarlet,' Jon said.

'It's worth the risk,' Huntly told him. 'You know you like her.'

'Scarlet thinks you don't rate her acting talent,' Mari said to Jon. 'But she says you've never seen her act in roles that make her shine.'

'She's probably, totally right,' Jon admitted. He took a deep breath. 'Okay, I'll let you two scallywags get back to eating your nosh and call Scarlet.'

And Jon was gone.

'Are you up for chocolate pudding?' Huntly said, lifting their empty dinner plates through to the kitchen.

'Oh, yes.'

She heard Huntly rustling around in the kitchen.

'With whipped cream or ice cream?' he called through to her.

'Yes, please.'

Huntly laughed and dished up two puddings with a scoop of chocolate ice cream and whipped cream.

He carried them through and put the plates down on the table. 'Tuck in.'

She did, enjoying the rich and delicious dessert.

'Niall and I are planning to add lights to the front of the theatre so that people notice us,' said Huntly. 'And Wil has agreed to perform at our theatre one evening with his new dance show. He's going to give us one of his posters to put in our front window.'

'I'll certainly buy a ticket to see that show.'

'You'll receive a complementary ticket. Unless Wil inveigles you to perform as one of the dancers,' he teased her.

Mari laughed. 'Eh, no, you want this dance show to be a success.'

Huntly smiled over at her, and she felt her heart react.

'I thought you waltzed beautifully,' he said. 'You certainly did when you were dancing with me.'

'You didn't see the faltering footwork going on underneath my dress. The ballgown hid a multitude.'

He gazed over at her, his handsome face highlighted in the glow of the candlelight. 'You were made for wearing a fairytale ballgown.'

She looked at the sparkle on the bodice of her dress glittering in the light. 'This is the first time I've worn a ballgown ever.'

'It won't be the last. There's a whirlwind of events coming up in the autumn and winter. Theatrical parties, dances, and the Christmas ball. Be prepared to dance your glass slippers off.'

Mari's heart soared with excitement. 'What a magical world you live in.'

'For us, it's real.' He leaned back and opened his arms wide, gesturing around him. 'And your world now too, remember.'

'I'm still at the pinching myself level.' She spooned up a mouthful of the rich chocolate pudding.

'No you're not,' he said firmly. 'We threw you in at the deep end the first day you came to the theatre to discuss your play. You've been sailing close to the wind with us ever since.'

'You and your sword are forged into my memory forever.'

He laughed. 'Apart from that faux pas though. You've adapted to all the things that have happened. You've even meddled in matchmaking Jon and Scarlet. Now that's quite an achievement.'

'I wonder how Jon's getting on with her. Do you think he'll have plucked up the nerve to call her?'

They were discussing this when a message came through on Huntly's phone. He grinned as he read it to Mari. 'Scarlet and I are having dinner tomorrow night.'

Mari smiled.

Huntly went to click his phone off, but saw he had another two messages. 'Mind if I check these? One is from the magazine journalist. The other is from a theatre director I know.'

Mari nodded and continued to finish her delicious pudding.

Huntly read the journalist's message. 'The first part of the magazine feature is online.' He hurried over to his laptop to access it.

'That was fast.'

'He worked as a newspaper journalist for the dailies, so he's used to writing to tight deadlines,' Huntly explained, skim–reading the editorial. 'It's mainly photos with captions. And he's gleaned information about the play from the synopsis. But he's written a nice piece about you.'

Mari went over and peered at the screen. There were several pictures of Huntly, Niall, Jon and Andy, along with ones of Wil dancing with Delphie.

'What does it say?' she said eagerly, her heart starting to race in anticipation.

Huntly read it, skipping over the parts about his theatre. '*A new play is due for an autumn release in the theatre. Intriguingly titled, The Shop That Sells Everything, it was written by a new and talented playwright.*'

Mari gasped, seeing a picture of herself wearing the jumper and skirt from earlier. 'Where did he get that photo? I don't remember it being taken.' It was flattering, but she was surprised to see it.

'Peter was taking photos of everyone as they arrived. He gave copies to the journalist. Nice picture of you.'

'It is...' The caption named her as Marigold, a new playwright. But in the editorial she'd been quoted as Mari.

Huntly continued to read. '*This is my first play to be performed,*' Mari said. '*I'm excited to be involved in the production, working with Jon the show's director and Andy acting in the lead role of Oglesby with a mysterious cat called Spindle.*'

Mari squeezed Huntly's arm. 'Oh my goodness. I've never been featured in a magazine before.' It was an involuntary touch, but she felt the lean muscles in his arm beneath his shirt. He still wore the brocade waistcoat, and in that moment, she felt a spark of attraction between them.

Huntly didn't make any move, but their faces were so close as they read the feature together, that he was sorely tempted to kiss her, even if only in the spur of the moment to congratulate her. But he didn't.

Mari took her hand away and then listened as he read on.

'I'm currently writing my next play and reworking previous material,' Mari said.

The remainder of the feature comprised of snippets from the synopsis revealing the play's storyline. And lots of pictures.

'There's one of us waltzing on stage,' he said.

Mari blinked, seeing herself in the beautiful ballgown, dancing with Huntly.

'We look as though we know what we're doing,' he said with a grin.

'My dress disguised a multitude of messy footwork.'

'Your posture is excellent,' he said.

'You held me in a vice–like grip of determined steel. I could hardly look otherwise,' she joked with him. 'Even dipping me.'

Huntly grabbed her playfully. 'Like this you mean?'

His gentle strength wrapped her in his arms and dipped her as if it was a dance finale.

She couldn't breathe for giggling. 'You're a rascal!'

Laughing, he righted her again, and dodged her swiping at him.

Catching the heel of her shoe on the hem of her dress, she almost took a tumble, but Huntly caught her in his capable arms, and as he pulled her close, that spark ignited again between them.

A spark of electric static shot through the air too, causing her to squeal, while Huntly fought all sorts of urges that he'd told himself he would not do. Dinner was as friends, to discuss business and chat about the theatre. Romance wasn't on the menu.

Clearing his thoughts, he spoke about the feature. 'It says that other parts of the interview feature are being published soon.'

'Oh, there's a video clip,' she said, noticing it at the top of the editorial.

Huntly clicked on it and they watched two minutes of Wil dancing with Mari, then with Huntly, Wil with Delphie, everyone on stage, including Niall, Jon and Andy.

He read the caption: '*Well–known dancer, Wil, and his dancers are performing his new dance show at the theatre for one special night. Tickets for the dance show and the new play will be available soon from the theatre.*'

Seeing the mention of tickets for sale made Mari's stomach flip with nerves. 'Everything is such a whirlwind.'

'You have to remember that we're working at a fast rate. Shows usually take months to prepare. So when you're working on your next play, you'll have time to take things at a more leisurely pace,' he assured her.

This brought the conversation full circle, back to the predicament of writing for other directors.

They'd barely touched on this, when two messages came through on Huntly's phone. One was a reminder from the director from earlier that he wanted to speak to him as a matter of urgency.

'Do you mind if I make a call to this director?' said Huntly.

'Go ahead,' she said, clearing the pudding dishes and taking them through to the kitchen to give him a modicum of privacy.

Huntly didn't want that. He followed her through while making the call, putting it on speaker so she could hear their conversation.

'I've been hearing about this new playwright you've snapped up, Huntly.'

Mari mouthed to Huntly. Tea?

He nodded, and she filled the kettle.

The theatre director continued. 'And I saw part of the magazine's online feature. She looks like a beautiful talent. I'm obviously interested in meeting her to discuss her writing something new for me.'

Mari glanced at Huntly, wondering what he would say, but before he could reply, the director spoke again.

'I assume you have first dibs on her next play.'

Mari nodded to Huntly, but he shook his head.

'No, not at all,' Huntly insisted, causing Mari to frown at him.

'Okay, then, can you pass on my name, number and desire to speak to her when she has her next play available for reading?'

'I'll will,' Huntly agreed, and the call ended shortly after that.

Mari set the cups up for the tea. 'I don't understand. I thought you'd be interested in seeing my new work.'

'I am. So don't get me wrong. I'd love first dibs on all your new plays. But that's not wise for you. Imagine if you were introduced to a director and they said they'd like to read the first ten pages of something new you were writing. And what if you hadn't shown it yet to Niall or me? You can't be running to us to ask permission first to show your work to others.'

Now she understood. 'And you're okay with that?'

'I want you to be a regular part of my theatre, but it's nonsensical to stifle your creativity. I hope we can continue to work closely. But I don't think you can build trust with shackles.'

Mari nodded, liking Huntly's openness more than she wanted to say. Liking Huntly more than was good for either of them.

He stepped close and gazed down at her. 'It's like romance. It complicates everything.'

Mari nodded again, not entirely wanting to agree, and poured their tea. She handed him a cup.

He raised it in a cheers. 'Not quite the champagne toast I had in mind.'

'I'm happy with tea.'

Was she happy with him, he wondered, fighting against the clash of feelings surging through him.

'To us, to your new play, to your wishes coming true.'

Mari tipped her cup against his in a toast, and almost spilled her tea when a flash of lightning lit up the night sky like nature's fireworks.

'A sign of things to come?' he said tentatively.

'Maybe,' she said softly. But the sparks of attraction running through her heart warned her to be careful.

CHAPTER ELEVEN

The spectacular view of Edinburgh enticed Mari to stay longer with Huntly, and the thunderstorm had faded into the night, leaving the sky a calm blue sprinkled with stars. But the evening was wearing on, and she was still dressed as if she belonged in a fairytale.

They were sitting in the living room, forgetting the time, steeped in conversation about the theatre, classic plays of yesteryear, Huntly's plans for forthcoming shows for the winter and Christmas, and Mari's eagerness to work on her new plays.

'Thank you for dinner,' Mari said, standing up. 'But it's getting late. I should change out of this ballgown.'

Huntly nodded, realising it was approaching midnight, and then he looked thoughtful. They'd been so engrossed in talking about other things that he hadn't had a chance to gauge her reaction to something special.

'Before you go, how about a song?' He stood up and gazed down at her looking hopeful.

Mari laughed lightly. 'My dancing is far better than my singing.'

He smiled. 'No, what I mean is...I've been offered a song for the play, written by a composer. It's a new piece he's written. A modern classic.'

She looked interested. 'Like a theme song for the play?'

'Yes. He came to the theatre this morning and played it on our piano. He's an excellent musician, and trying to place his material where his work will be showcased. Niall and I think it's viable. The play isn't a musical, but a theme song would be a way to add to the atmosphere and the drama for the opening scene and as a crescendo when the play finishes.'

'I'm inclined to say yes, but I'd obviously love to hear it first.'

Huntly frowned. 'He didn't leave a recording of the song. He just played it for us on the piano. But he did leave a copy of the music. It's downstairs in the office. Come on, I have an idea.'

Clasping Mari's hand, he led her outside, taking the scenic route again. 'I thought you'd like another look at the view.'

They paused again to admire the lights glistening all around them.

The heady autumn air blew gently through the fabric of her dress, and she breathed in the beauty of the night.

Huntly's tall, broad shouldered stature shielded her from the cold, but then he hurried her down the stairs and into the warmth of the theatre. They had it all to themselves.

'I'll get changed,' Mari said, heading through to the wardrobe area. 'And I'll show you the knitted black cat pattern I brought with me.'

'Great, I'll pick up the sheet of music from the office and meet you back at the piano.'

They headed away in different directions.

Pockets of lighting illuminated the theatre and created an atmosphere that felt warm and shielded from the outside world.

In a trail of sparkling chiffon, Mari hurried backstage and along to wardrobe, past the rails of costumes to the changing area.

Mari found her jumper and skirt neatly folded where Heather had left them there for her, along with her bag. The knitted black cat's face peered over the top of the bag, its green eyes stitched on with yarn.

She managed to unfasten the back of her ballgown and stepped out of the most beautiful dress she'd ever worn.

Quickly putting her clothes on, she picked up her bag.

Hanging the dress up on a rail, she headed back through to the heart of the theatre.

The baby grand piano was set up at an area at the side, and was lit by a spotlight. The lid was propped up ready for playing.

Huntly stood beside it, pouring over the sheet music, rehearsing it in his mind.

'Are you going to play the song?' Mari said, sounding excited.

'I'll give it a go.' He sat down on the piano stool and put the sheet music on the stand.

Mari settled into one of the front row seats. The theatre was so silent she imagined she could hear her eagerly beating heart.

And then Huntly started to play the dramatic opening notes, filling the theatre with the melodic music.

It was a magnificent modern classical piece, and she knew as soon as she heard it that it was perfect for the show.

But her heart was enthralled too by Huntly's playing, his skill as a pianist.

The wonderful rich tones from the baby grand piano rose to a triumphant crescendo, resonating in the theatre, and lingered for a moment after Huntly had lifted his hands off the keys.

'I love the song, and you play it so well,' she said, walking over to stand at the side of the piano.

'We'll include it as part of the show. I'll contact the composer.'

'Will you play the song?'

'No, the composer is a marvellous pianist. He'll record it in a studio. We'll play the recording of the song during each performance.'

'I should've recorded you playing it,' she said. 'That would've been a highlight for the archives.'

'The theatre's acoustics are excellent. Sometimes, when I've locked up the theatre for the night, and everyone has gone home, I indulge in playing the piano. A favourite rhapsody or concerto.' He tapped the stool. 'I keep a selection of sheet music tucked inside the seat's handy storage unit.'

Mari pictured Huntly sitting there on his own playing into the night.

Huntly continued. 'I have a baby grand piano at my house in Edinburgh, but I'm so busy these days I rarely have time to play it.' He swept his fingers lightly across the piano keys. 'This let's me keep my hand in at least.'

'You play beautifully,' she said, still feeling the tingles from his performance.

'Do you play at all?'

'No, but it must be a wonderful feeling to sit down and play like you did,' she said wistfully.

Huntly moved to one side of the piano stool. 'Sit down and play a few notes.'

Mari hesitated, but was tempted.

'Come on,' he said.

She sat down beside him, and he gently instructed her, placing her hands on the keys.

Her heartbeat increased from his closeness, the touch of his hands on hers, as he showed her the technique for her hand position.

'Relax,' he instructed her. 'Let your fingers gently drop down on to the keys. Not too hard.'

She felt the notes resonate beneath her fingers, and smiled as Huntly helped her to play a few more notes.

'Breathe, don't hold your breath,' he told her.

She tried to follow his instructions, but she kept catching her breath from the sheer excitement of sitting there with Huntly trying to follow his lead.

Finally, she lifted her hands away. 'Thank you for my first ever piano lesson. Though I think I'll stick to writing.'

'And knitting,' he reminded her. 'Didn't you say you had a pattern to show me?'

'I do.' She stood up and went over to where she'd left her bag.

Huntly followed her.

'Everyone in my class today at the craft shop enjoyed knitting the pattern,' she said, giving him a copy of it. 'It's easy to knit.'

Huntly read the instructions. 'I'll take your word for it.'

'Can you knit at all?' she said.

'Not a stitch. I've no idea how to cast on and knit rows,' he said, reading the instructions. 'But I like the look of the pattern.'

'Ivy made up this sample bag to show you how the kit could be sold.'

Huntly peered in the paper bag.

'It contains a copy of the pattern, a picture of the finished cat, the yarn and a knitters sewing needle for stitching the seams together with yarn, and to sew the eyes, nose and whiskers,' she explained. 'And soft filler to stuff the cat.'

'So there would be everything you need in the one bag,' he said.

'Yes, and a pair of basic knitting needles could be included, depending on how you want to cost it.'

Huntly lifted up the cat she'd knitted. 'He's got character. I like him.'

'I adapted a pattern I had, and I think it works well.'

'Can I keep this kit to show Niall in the morning?'

'Yes, I brought it to give to you.'

'Ideal.' Then he grinned at her. 'I noticed that Ivy's shop window had knitted cats on display. I was going by this morning when I popped out to buy groceries for our dinner.'

'Yes, and customers are having fun making them.'

He checked the time, then picked up the knitted cat, the sample pattern bag with the yarn, and the new song's sheet music. 'I'll put these in the office and then walk you home.'

'You don't have to do that,' she said, knowing he would insist. Deep in her heart she liked that he wanted to see her home.

Huntly hurried away to the office. 'Wait here. There's something I promised I'd show you.'

She waited, wondering what he had in mind.

Dropping the items in the office, he walked back down to join her. 'You wanted to know how to open the wrought iron gate at the old entrance to the theatre.'

'The gate with no key and no lock.'

'There's a knack to it. We'll leave through that route and I'll show you.'

Huntly switched the lights off behind them as they walked through the corridors leading to wardrobe and then to the exit door.

The night air wafted in as he pushed it open.

Mari's jumper kept her warm as she followed Huntly along the narrow pathway at the side of the theatre. Everything was cast in shadows and light, but she felt a sense of excitement in the air, that they were out so late at night, up to mischief.

He stopped in front of the securely closed gate. A dim light shone a glow so she could see what he was doing.

'Give me your bag,' he said.

She handed it to him.

'Now put your hands through this gap here, between the bars.'

Mari did as he instructed.

Hoisting her bag up on to his shoulder, he guided her hands. 'Twist and turn your hands and wrists like this, while pressing against this part of the hidden mechanism.'

Click. The gate opened.

'It worked!' she said.

'Right, now once we're through, just pull the gate shut behind you. You'll hear it lock again.'

They stepped through and Mari closed the gate behind them.

Another click sounded in the quiet of the night.

'That's very handy,' she told him.

'Hopefully you won't need to use it like we did when we were running away.'

'No, but considering the drama you create, it's handy to know the knack,' she said, taking her bag from him.

The narrow pathway took them to the front of the theatre.

He glanced up at it. 'Work starts tomorrow morning on the lights. We're going to add them around the theatre sign and on the edges of a new canopy. We'll take pictures and update our website with our new look.'

Mari pictured it all aglow in the night, and people queuing to get into the theatre to see the shows.

Then they started to walk down the street.

'Will you be going back to your private turret?' she said lightly.

'Yes, I've an early start in the morning. Sammy and Peter are helping organise the new lights for the front of the theatre. So be prepared for some razzle dazzle.'

'You seem to spend little time in your house,' she remarked.

'I'm planning to balance things better. It's just such a crazy busy time. I miss relaxing at home though. I like pottering around in my garden. The flowers are still looking lovely, lingering from the summer blooms, lots of roses, gardenia, gerbera and I have sunflowers.'

'I love flowers, and would like a garden again one day. The flat is great, but it obviously doesn't have a proper garden.'

'Come and have dinner with me at my house one evening and have a potter around the plants.'

'Is this a ruse to get me to tame your garden for you?' she joked.

He played along. 'Ah, you caught me out.'

She wanted to take him up on his offer that dangled enticingly in the air.

'But do come round for dinner,' he said. 'We'll arrange a date that suits us.'

'Okay, I'd like that.'

They walked on, chatting.

He brought up the subject of dating, and she deftly avoided going into the tedious details of splitting up with her ex–boyfriend. 'I'm not one for digging up my past romantic disasters as there's little to find except weeds.'

Huntly nodded. 'I've been called a reluctant romantic, though I'd argue that I'm more unlucky in love than an avoider of it.'

'It's a good job we've both decided to put romance on the back burner to concentrate on our work.'

'Yes,' he heard himself agree, while feeling the truth fighting to be heard.

He'd enjoyed having dinner with Mari, and his entire evening had been brightened by her company. It was hard to recall a time when he'd had more fun and felt satisfied just dining and chatting.

They'd dealt with a lot of business, having time to discuss various matters without the inevitable interruptions of the theatre, and he felt he knew her a little better, but this only caused his interest in her to rise to a level where he was sorely tempted to ask her out on a proper date.

But he heeded his own warning not to do it. In the cold light of day he'd regret wasting what had been a memorable evening.

'Are you taking any knitting classes tomorrow?' he said as they walked down towards the craft shop. Ivy had left a little string of twinkle lights on in the window display and it acted like a beacon guiding their way to Mari's flat.

'No, but I'm planning to catch up on my knitting, and I'm particularly excited to do some writing. Unless you need me at the theatre.'

'There's nothing urgent planned,' he said. 'Make your own hours to suit your work. I'll call if anything requires your involvement. Or if there's another drama I've created or become involved in.'

'I'll expect to hear from you in the morning, afternoon and evening then,' she said.

Huntly's laughter sounded in the quiet street. 'You have my measure now, don't you.'

'Oh, I'm not sure about that. You're a man just full of surprises.'

'Fun ones, I hope.'

'Yes, and I'm still impressed with your piano playing.'

'I don't usually play specifically for anyone.'

'I'm flattered you played for me. Though I understand you wanted me to hear the new song so you could decide whether to include it in the show.'

'The gossip is going to spark, and people will say I was serenading you.' This wasn't so far from the truth.

'I won't tell anyone you played if you won't,' she said.

Huntly shook his head. 'They'll find out. There are no secrets in the theatre.'

'I quite like that. Everything out in the open. Though I'm anxious about being pictured in part two of the magazine feature.'

Huntly gestured as if it was a headline. 'Marigold goes wild in the theatre. Playwright's secret passion for waltzing.'

Clasping her in his arms, Huntly began whirling her across the cobbles.

Her laughter resonated in the quietude as he spun and whirled her down the street and stopped outside the close beside the craft shop.

For one breathless moment, she thought he was going to kiss her, and she couldn't have promised that she would've resisted him.

But instead of compromising her, he let her go and stepped back, though still near enough to remain a temptation to her wandering thoughts.

Mari gathered herself and shrugged her bag back up on to her shoulder. 'You're a scoundrel.'

Huntly laughed.

Mari cast him a smile and then headed through the close and up the stairs to her flat.

Huntly went with her and waited until she'd jiggled her key in the lock and opened the door.

'It's finicky,' she said.

'You know the knack though. And how to open the old gate at the side of the theatre.'

'Yes, so now you won't be able to hide from me in the theatre. I know the secret way in.'

For a moment, his face looked sensual and serious. 'I'd never want to hide from you, Mari.'

Then he stepped back from his own temptation.

'So, I'll call you tomorrow then with whatever mischief and mayhem I've stirred up.'

He heard her laughing as he walked away, ending one of the best nights he'd had in a long time.

Walking back up to the theatre, he thought about the offer he'd made that she'd accepted. Dinner at his house. A mistake, or a chance to deepen their friendship?

He hadn't figured out an answer by the time he'd reached the theatre. Glancing up at the entrance, he pictured it would soon be all lit up with lights. The early start didn't seem daunting. He was eager to help get the work done. It was time to shine and promote the theatre.

Upstairs in his bolthole, he stripped off and got ready for bed. Wandering through in his dark silk shorts to the living room to turn the lights off, he noticed his laptop was lit up with messages. People had seen the online feature.

He sat down and quickly replied to them, offering invitations to some to attend the opening night of the play, adding details to others, responding to all the messages from friends and acquaintances.

One message was from a radio interviewer inviting him and Niall on to the show to talk about the play. He confirmed his interest in this and mentioned about having a theme song, something he thought would be ideal for the radio interview.

Dealing with all the messages, he closed the laptop and headed through to bed.

Lying there, gazing out at the view of the city at night, he rewound his evening with Mari. His heart reacted just thinking about her.

From all the messages he'd received, he knew she was bound to have been contacted too, about her playwriting.

During the evening, she'd spoken about the other plays she'd written. Two and a half to be precise. The storylines were all different, and he'd told her he was interested in reading them when she felt they were ready. Even the half finished one sounded exciting and intriguing. But he'd made it clear that she was free to show other directors too.

Forcing himself to get some sleep, he drifted off, wondering what drama he'd attract in the busy day ahead.

CHAPTER TWELVE

Mari sat up in bed reading the opening scenes to one of her plays on her laptop.

She knew she should be sensible and get some sleep. But she felt unsettled and eager to work on her writing. As she made her own hours and didn't have any knitting class to teach the next day, she decided to make a cup of tea and sit up, snug in bed, working on the storyline.

She'd received a message from Scarlet's director expressing his interest in her writing a Christmas play for him. At first, she thought he meant for the coming Christmas, but no, he was talking about next Christmas. He planned his theatre schedule seasons ahead, so she'd replied and agreed to meet with him if she wrote a festive play.

Huntly kept crossing her mind, but she tried to concentrate on her writing, adding to the dialogue of the main characters. A rich romantic thread ran through this particular play, and she was in the mood for writing romance.

This story was set in the past, a vintage piece, that she pictured with wonderful costumes from the era. She'd seen costumes hanging up in the theatre's wardrobe collection. Vintage dresses and suits hanging on the rails. Not that she was sure Huntly would want to accept this play, but it helped fire up her imagination, creating a world that would look vibrant and atmospheric on stage.

She'd learned a lot recently from working with Huntly and the others in the theatre. Seeing how the sets were built, starry night skies created with the lighting, the props, and Heather's dressmaking skills making the costumes, helped her to write with these things in mind. The play she'd written could be so much more than she'd originally planned.

Taking a sip of her tea, she started rewriting late into the night.

'Put the lights all the way along the canopy,' Huntly said, standing in front of the theatre the next morning. The sky was a pale blue with amber sunshine, and the colourful lights were due to further brighten the day.

Crew were bustling around, up ladders, putting the finishing touches to the lights around the theatre's sign and dotted on the edges of the canopy, creating a welcoming glow.

The ticket banner was in the window and the new play advertised. Huntly felt the excitement building.

The other shows on their schedule were almost ready to run, and their dress rehearsals were imminent. He was confident these would be popular. But he had a feeling about Mari's play being a huge success. And he wasn't the only one. Jon sensed it too, as did Andy and others.

'That looks great,' Huntly called up to the crew. 'A wonderful job.'

Huntly was admiring the colourful lights when Heather came hurrying out of the theatre.

'Niall's got the cat's yarn in a fankle,' said Heather. 'I'm just running down to the craft shop to buy another ball.'

'Let me go,' Huntly insisted.

Looking mildly harassed, Heather was happy to take Huntly up on his offer. 'Ivy knows what type of black yarn we need. She'll keep you right.' And off she ran back into the theatre.

Huntly strode down to the craft shop, picturing the chaos that Niall had caused. Peter had borrowed a set of knitting needles from Heather and wanted to try knitting the cat. Peter wasn't a skilled knitter, but he'd learned to knit blanket squares when he was at school, and thought he could tackle the pattern with Heather's help to cast on the stitches.

Niall remembered learning to knit squares at school too, though his recollections weren't up to Peter's prop–making standards. Chaos had been created when Niall wanted to knit a couple of rows of the pattern before Peter started to decrease the stitches to shape the cat's head.

Nothing had gone right for Niall, and even Heather's unpicking skills couldn't get the tangled mess under control. It was easier to snip the knotted part out and rejoin the yarn. But now there was a lot less to work with. How Niall had wasted so much she couldn't imagine.

Mari had popped out for Scottish morning rolls for her breakfast. She had a notion of a roll and butter and a nice cup of tea.

The early morning had been a flurry of activity dealing with a handful of customer orders, and organising her day so she could work on her writing and her knitting. Despite the late night, she was looking forward to a cosy day in her flat.

Wearing a colourful patterned knitted waistcoat over her blouse, and her cinnamon cords, she blended with the burnished bronze tones of the nearby trees and greenery. The scent of autumn filled the air as she picked up her rolls and walked back home.

Amber sunlight obscured her view of the craft shop as she walked towards it, heading for her close.

Was that Huntly hurrying into the shop?

Squinting against the glow, the tall, manly figure had gone. Shrugging away her surprise, she put it down to the effect of the sunlight, and headed into the close and up to her flat to make breakfast.

Ivy wasn't surprised as Huntly rushed in, looking dashing in the Aran jumper Mari had knitted for him and expensive dark trousers. She'd seen knitwear models like him, though she made no comment.

'Here's the black yarn you need,' Ivy said as he approached the counter. Off his surprised look, she explained, 'Heather phoned to say you were on your way due to an emergency fankle caused by Niall.'

That about summed it up, so he didn't bother with the details, and accepted the bag that had three balls of black yarn.

'Three?' he said, peeking in the bag.

'Just in case anyone else takes a notion to knit a cat.'

'Thank you, Ivy.' He put more than enough money down to pay for it.

'Before you go, I made up another sample bag for you to take with you.'

Huntly grabbed that too and went to add to the payment.

'You've more than covered the cost,' Ivy told him. And then she took a breath and spoke up. 'I took the liberty of costing the cat pattern package.' Slipping a piece of paper with the numbers she'd calculated for a bulk order of the kits, she waited to see if his reaction was favourable or if she'd overstepped.

Huntly lifted the sheet of paper that was neatly typed and itemised with a breakdown on the options. 'This is so helpful, Ivy.' He ran his finger along the items and nodded. 'Fair, economical, practical but profitable for both of us.'

'I don't mean to be pushy, but it seems as if you're interested in the kit, so I'm used to pricing these for my shop and—'

'I'm delighted,' Huntly cut–in. 'I'll take this with me, confirm it with Niall and call you later today.'

'I've given two options,' Ivy explained, pointing to the paper. 'One doesn't include knitting needles, and one does but costs a wee bit more.'

'Given that Peter and Niall had to wangle a pair from Heather, I'd say the latter is our best bet.'

'That's what I would advise,' Ivy agreed. 'The needles are the type I buy in for beginners. They're shorter and great to get you started, and they'll knit up the cat perfectly. It doesn't take many stitches on each row. Experienced knitters will have their own needles, and Mari designed it with a standard, popular size. But I find that my customers love these sets of knitting needles and like to buy them to add to their collections.'

'Let's go with the kit that includes a set of the knitting needles,' said Huntly.

Ivy was waving Huntly off when Bob came bustling in. 'Morning there, Huntly. I'm Bob, Ivy's husband. I baked your celebration cake recently.'

Huntly went to shake his hand, but Bob was carrying a white cardboard cake box with a selection of sticky buns, tattie scones and an oatmeal loaf for Ivy. Bob balanced the box anyway and shook hands.

'Your cakes are delicious,' said Huntly.

'I hear you're a bit of a baker yourself.' Bob winked knowingly.

'I dabble,' Huntly said, then eyed the large sticky buns, glistening with an icing glaze, raisins, sugared fruits and glacé cherries.

'Help yourself.' Bob offered up the box and Huntly accepted one. He hadn't had breakfast, just a slurp of tea, before his hectic day had started.

I see you're putting up a show of lights on your theatre,' said Bob. 'They're looking grand.'

'Lights on the theatre,' Ivy exclaimed. 'That'll catch people's attention.'

'That's the plan,' said Huntly, eager to head back to the theatre, and to take a bite of the sticky bun.

Bob stepped aside. 'I won't hold you up, Huntly. Enjoy your bun.'

'Thanks again,' Huntly called to Ivy, smiled at Bob, and then dashed back up the street to the theatre.

There was nothing left except sticky fingers by the time he arrived outside the theatre. The crew had finished the lighting task, the ladders were gone, and everything looked aglow with the pretty lights. It wasn't too gaudy or ostentatious, and reminded him of theatre lights he'd seen from bygone days.

Heading inside the foyer, he almost bumped into a couple of people on their way out. Several others were queuing at the box office to buy tickets for the shows, especially for Mari's play.

A member of staff was busy attending to the ticket sales for the advance bookings, and smiled over at Huntly as he went by into the office.

'Ticket sales have soared,' Niall said as Huntly walked in. 'For the new play, and our other shows. Word is getting around. And that's before we light the theatre up like a beacon tonight.'

'Wonderful!' said Huntly.

'I'm sorry about the kerfuffle I caused with the knitting,' Niall apologised.

Huntly put the replacement yarn down on the desk. 'Ivy to the rescue with replenishments.' He showed Niall her suggestion for costing the kit.

Niall read it over and nodded. 'This seems fair to me.'

'I'll call Ivy and confirm that she should order in the materials we need,' said Huntly.

Peter interrupted, popping into the office. 'Heather says Ivy gave you more of the black wool so I can finish the cat.'

'Here you go.' Huntly handed him the spare bag of yarn, leaving the new sample bag on the desk.

'Do you want to help me stuff the cat when I've finished knitting it?' Peter offered to Niall.

'I'll forgo that pleasure,' Niall told him.

'Okay,' said Peter, and then headed away happily with the replacement yarn.

'I contacted the composer,' Huntly told Niall. 'He's booking a session at a recording studio, but he wants to know whether to add harp accents to the song. He says it'll work well with the violin, guitar and piano.'

'Harp sounds lovely to me,' said Niall.

Huntly sent a message to the composer confirming that they liked the idea of the harp. 'There, that'll let him plan what he needs for the recording. And he's excited about the song being played during our radio interview.'

Niall rubbed his hands together. 'I don't know about you, but I'm famished. I skipped breakfast. Will I grab something tasty for us from the cafe?'

'Phone Bob, he's out doing his bakery rounds. I can recommend the sticky buns.'

'Sounds tasty. Bob bakes our celebration cakes doesn't he? I should have his number here.' He flicked through the list of contacts on his phone.

Leaving Niall to phone Bob, Huntly called Ivy giving her the go ahead to order what they needed for a batch of the kits.

'I'm on it,' said Ivy. 'Leave it with me. I'll sort out all the kits you'll need. For round one anyway. If they sell like hotcakes, I'll make up some more.'

'Thanks, Ivy, you're such a great help. Bill me for everything,' Huntly told her. 'And would you please make sure that Mari's name and logo are included as the pattern designer, and your name and craft shop's logo as the materials supplier.'

'Oh, yes, I'll do that.' Ivy was delighted. She hadn't expected her shop to be included.

Mari drank her tea and ate her tasty buttered roll for breakfast while reading through the play she'd been rewriting the previous night. She sat cosy in the quietude of her living room with her laptop set up on her work table.

Steeped in her story, she read up to the part where she'd finished rewriting, and then continued reading while picking up a vest she'd been knitting. The pattern was a mix of soft neutral colours with hints of rich burgundy. She knitted while reading through the second act of the play, barely making any changes to the writing.

Working on two things at the one time wasn't what she planned to do on a regular basis, but it allowed her to catch up on her knitting while making progress with the play. Often she'd watch a film or read something on her laptop while she was knitting, so she was quite used to the duality of her current working method. But she knew there would come a point where she had to choose one as her priority, and with the interest building in her plays it seemed apparent that her dream of being a playwright would win the day.

Huntly hadn't interrupted her with any messages, so she assumed his morning had run smoothly, and she was looking forward to seeing the new lights up on the theatre.

A drama–free day was what they both needed. Life didn't always have to imitate art, even though she was reading through a dramatic second act of her play.

Bob delivered their bakery order of sticky buns, tattie scones, Scottish pancakes and cheese pastries, bringing it on a tray to the theatre's office.

'Here you go, lads,' Bob said cheerily, setting the items down on their desk.

'Everything smells delicious,' said Huntly, grabbing two plates from beside their tea making table.

'I've brought some wee extras to tempt your taste buds.' Bob then added a slice of apple bread, a buttermilk scone and a raspberry muffin. He'd included little pats of butter and jam.

Niall felt his stomach rumble hungrily just looking at the array of bakery treats. 'This will keep us going all day. Thanks, Bob.'

Happy that they were delighted, Bob glanced around at the show posters and pictures of the theatre on the office walls. 'So this is what your theatre looks like inside. I've never been to any of your shows, but I'm certainly going to be frequenting it now. It's a lot bigger and grander than the impression I had from outside.'

By now, Huntly had flicked the kettle on to boil and was setting up the tea cups.

'Have a donner around if you want,' Huntly said to Bob, gesturing that he was free to have a look around.

'I'll just have a wee peek to see the stage and the seating. Is that a balcony you have too?' Bob said, studying one of the pictures.

'It is,' Niall told him.

Heather popped into the office. 'Thanks for getting the extra yarn. Peter was eager to finish knitting the pattern and then stuff the cat.'

'No need to explain, lads,' Bob said to Huntly and Niall, seeing their reaction to Heather's remark. 'I'm up to speed on the fankle fiasco. Ivy told me.'

'If you're not too busy, Heather, would you like to show Bob around the theatre,' said Huntly.

Heather knew Bob well and linked her arm through his. 'Leave your baking board in the foyer and come with me. I'll give you a tour of wardrobe and backstage.'

Being whisked away by Heather, Bob called back to them. 'If I'm not back by teatime, send out a search party.'

'He has no idea how close he is to that being true,' Niall muttered, biting into a cheese pastry.

Huntly grinned, and was pouring their tea when Jon wandered in looking ruffled rather than his usual suave self.

'You look like you've been wrestling monsters in your sleep,' Huntly remarked, pouring a third cup of tea.

Jon flopped down on the nearest chair, didn't blink at the array of bakery goods on the desk, helped himself to a sticky bun and bit into it.

'Like that, is it?' Huntly said to him.

Jon nodded and munched on the bun, seemingly oblivious to what it was. 'I skipped breakfast and lunch,' he muttered, enjoying the sweet, sticky sustenance.

'It's still morning, Jon,' Huntly enlightened him.

Jon threw a couldn't care less gesture at him, still gripping what was left of the bun.

'What did Scarlet do to you?' Niall said to Jon.

'Nothing, *yet*.' Jon's emphasis on the time scale indicated part of his problem.

Huntly put a cup of tea down in front of him.

The three of them sat down around the desk drinking their tea and tucking into the buns, pastries, scones and pancakes. Huntly and Niall added butter and jam to some of theirs.

Jon was still looking distraught and dishevelled. He took another bite of the bun, washed it down with a swig of tea, and then reeled off his concerns of stepping into the jaws of the dating game with Scarlet.

'I live in a world of fiction, of plays, of characters and drama,' Jon began. 'But as the director, I'm in control of that.' He shook his head and took another slurp of tea. 'Romance, dating past girlfriends, never goes well or ends well in my real life.'

'You haven't even had dinner with Scarlet yet,' said Huntly.

'And that's the problem.' Jon sounded perturbed. 'I didn't think that a gorgeous woman like Scarlet would be interested in dating me. It's thrown me for a loop. I'm running round in circles trying to think where to take her for dinner so I can impress her. Or at least, not mess it up by booking a table in a restaurant she doesn't like.'

'Ask her where she'd like to have dinner.' This seemed like the easy solution to Niall.

'I did.' Jon's tone was heavy. 'She said she wants me to surprise her with somewhere wonderful. But we all know how fussy Scarlet is.'

Huntly and Niall nodded.

'Tricky,' Niall assessed.

'A complete conundrum,' said Jon. 'Andy says I should cook her a candlelit dinner at my house. But I can't cook for toffee. And it's too intimate a setting for our first date.'

'True,' Huntly agreed, thinking about this same issue now that he'd invited Mari to dinner at his house.

'I'm working myself up into a lather over nothing,' said Jon. 'Though it's everything. Scarlet and me becoming a couple...' He shook his head. 'I'd never have thought it. But what if it worked out? We're in the same business.'

Niall suggested a restaurant.

Jon sighed heavily. 'Fully booked for tonight. As are several others I thought she'd love.'

'What about that restaurant we all went to in the summer to celebrate one of our opening nights.' Huntly named the venue.

Jon's interest perked up. 'Yes! The food was fabulous, and it was such a romantic setting.' Grabbing his phone he called the restaurant. 'Fingers, toes and anything else crossed for me,' he said urgently to Huntly and Niall.

They gave him bolstering looks as he spoke to the restaurant. And then they heard him book a table for two, a window seat with a view of Edinburgh.

Jon clicked his phone off and punched the air. 'Nailed it! Thank you,' he said to them.

Huntly patted him on the back. 'Scarlet will love it.'

Niall nodded. 'Now all you have to do is be dashing, daring and her dream come true.'

Jon's usual suave self started to shine through his previous reticence. 'No problem.' Then he looked at what he'd been munching. 'What are we celebrating?'

'Stuff,' said Huntly with a casual shrug. 'And the lights are up outside the theatre.'

Jon blinked. 'Are they? I didn't notice them. Are they lit?'

'A blaze of vibrant colours,' said Huntly.

And then they all laughed.

'If this is what dating Scarlet has done to you before you've even had your first dinner together, I think you may have found the woman for you,' Huntly told Jon.

Jon nodded and buttered himself a pancake, then they discussed their busy day ahead over another round of tea.

'How did your dinner go last night with Mari?' Niall said to Huntly.

'Fine, we enjoyed our meal and chatted about her playwriting, the theatre, and I played the new song for her on the piano.'

Niall and Jon exchanged a glance.

'You serenaded her,' said Niall.

'No, she wanted to hear the new song, so I played it.'

'Are we including the song in the play?' Jon wanted to know.

'Yes, the composer is recording it for us,' said Huntly. 'It'll be ideal as part of the radio interview.'

'The second part of the magazine feature is online now,' Niall told them.

'Is it?' Huntly checked it on his phone. 'What does it say?'

'There are more details about the play,' said Niall. 'More pictures of all of us, and a bit about Wil performing at the theatre.'

Jon read it on his phone too. 'This is excellent publicity. And that's a lovely picture of you smiling at Mari.'

Huntly looked at the picture and his heart melted a little seeing her smiling at him too.

'I've inadvertently invited Mari to have dinner one night at my house,' Huntly told them.

Jon smirked. 'You fox.'

'No, just as friends,' Huntly clarified. 'It was late last night and I was walking her home and I sort of invited her to dinner.'

Niall and Jon exchanged a knowing look.

'I think you may have found the woman for you too,' Jon said to Huntly.

Huntly shook his head. 'No, romance would complicate everything.'

Peter popped into the office and held up the knitted cat he'd made. 'He's finished, and I've added a pipe cleaner into his tail.' Peter showed them the different angles the tail could be set to. 'Nifty, isn't it.'

'Great job,' said Huntly.

The others were equally enthusiastic.

Peter propped the cat up on a shelf and adjusted the tail to an upright position. Nodding that he was pleased with his handiwork, he hurried away again.

'I can't knit a stitch, but even I have a notion to knit a woolly cat,' Jon admitted. Then he looked at Niall. 'Didn't you say that you could knit?'

Niall looked awkward.

Huntly took a deep breath and smiled. 'Well...'

CHAPTER THIRTEEN

'So it was Huntly I saw dashing into your shop this morning,' Mari said, hearing what had happened from Ivy.

Mari had gone down to the craft shop to hand in a few parcels for delivery to her customers. Her stock was running low, but she still had some items available, including the vests, woolly hats and scarves. And she was working on a couple of jumpers, along with the one Niall had ordered. She'd made Niall's jumper a priority and it was already almost finished.

'Yes, and Huntly has ordered a large batch of the knitted cat kits for the theatre.' Ivy had been busy assembling them when Mari had walked in.

'You should've told me. I'd have come down and helped you make up the bags.'

'You need time to work on your writing.'

'It's a lot of work to do by yourself,' said Mari.

'Och, wheesht, I've got my wee production line going.' Ivy gestured to the numerous bags she'd already made. 'I've been making up craft kits for years. It's a skoosh. I enjoy it, and I've got all the contents I need from my storeroom through the back. And I've ordered in extra sets of knitting needles that'll arrive tomorrow morning so I can finish the first big order.'

Mari sighed. 'I'm going to have to give priority, at least for a wee while, to my writing. I'll still teach the knitting classes, but there aren't enough hours in the day to do everything.'

'You don't want to run yourself ragged,' said Ivy. 'Playwriting should be your priority. I appreciate you continuing with the classes. But you'll need to reduce the items you knit for sale.'

Mari nodded. 'My work with the theatre has been more exciting, but time consuming, than I'd thought. But Huntly hasn't contacted me today, so I assume after the fiasco with Niall's knotted knitting, things have run smoothly.'

As she said this, Huntly phoned Mari.

'I spoke too soon,' she said to Ivy and then took the call.

'Can you come up to the theatre?' Huntly's tone sounded urgent.

'Yes, is something wrong?'

'A photo–journalist dropped by. He wants to do a quick interview for tomorrow's paper. And take some press photos of us outside the theatre.'

'I'm on my way.' She clicked the call off and turned to Ivy. 'Huntly wants me to be part of a press interview.'

'Go for it,' Ivy encouraged her.

Giving her hair a brush through and putting on her lipstick, Mari hurried out of the craft shop and up to the theatre. A burnished sun was punching through the clouds, and she hoped it would shine long enough while the photos were taken.

Her heart was fluttering as she reached the theatre and went inside.

Huntly and Niall were coming out of the office, chatting to the photo–journalist.

Bob's bread board had vanished from the foyer, so Huntly assumed that the boisterous baker had made it back from the depths of the wardrobe and backstage tour to continue his day of delivering cakes and sticky buns.

Wil's dance poster had arrived by courier and Peter had pinned it up in one of the front windows, so Huntly was confident that the theatre would look great for the photo–shoot.

The photo–journalist recognised Mari immediately from the pictures he'd seen online and greeted her with a smile. 'Marigold. Pleased to meet you. I'm interested in chatting about your new play. But can we all head outside and get the pics in the bag first.'

Niall led the way.

Huntly whispered to Mari. 'Thanks for dashing up. He dropped by hoping to make this evening's deadline for the paper.'

'It's fine,' Mari assured him, feeling the fluttering of her heart increase as they all stepped outside.

'Could the three of you stand at the front entrance, with Marigold in the middle.' The photo–journalist adjusted his camera and started taking pictures as they posed together.

'I'll tell him you prefer to be called Mari,' Huntly whispered to her.

She nodded while smiling for the camera.

'The lights make a huge difference to the theatre,' the photo–journalist remarked. 'Are Jon and Andy joining us?'

'Here we are,' Andy said, hurrying out of the theatre with Jon.

Lots more photos were taken.

Satisfied he had all the pictures he needed, the photo–journalist headed back inside to get some quotes from them all, having read the copy of the play's synopsis that Huntly had given him. He was particularly interested in talking to Mari about her playwriting, and he'd interviewed the others during times in the past. His aim was to glean an exclusive for the paper.

Mari kept her comments succinct, relevant to her writing, but she was pressed to include information about her knitting and that she'd moved to Edinburgh from the town up the coast.

Huntly wanted to protect her from the onslaught of prying questions, but Mari was well capable of speaking up for herself, and he knew she'd have to get used to being in the limelight.

The photo–journalist finished the interview with more photos, this time showing Mari standing holding the knitted cat she'd made alongside Andy, wearing his costume and posing with Fluffy.

'Right, I'll go and get this written up for the deadline. It'll be in tomorrow's edition of the paper.' Waving, the photo–journalist left the theatre.

'Phew!' said Mari. 'That was intense.'

'You did great,' Andy told her.

The others agreed.

Huntly stepped closer to her. 'You really did.'

Mari smiled at him, and felt the knots in her stomach start to unwind.

Jon checked the time. 'I'm off to get ready for dinner with Scarlet.'

'Have fun,' Huntly said to Jon.

Everyone peeled off in different directions. Jon hurried away for his dinner date, Andy headed through to wardrobe to change out of his costume and tuck Fluffy back in props, Niall had a business call to make and walked back to the office, and Mari sat the knitted cat on the display they'd set up in the theatre's shop in the foyer. Huntly watched her, wondering when he should make that date for dinner at his house.

'Mari,' Huntly called to her, as she was leaving.

She turned and looked round at him.

Huntly walked towards her. 'Are you busy this evening?'

'I've nothing special planned. Was there something you wanted me to do?'

'I wondered if you'd like to have dinner at my house.' He was aware that it was an impromptu invitation, and was prepared for her refusal or polite excuse to keep this for another time.

'Okay,' she heard herself accept. There was no specific reason why she shouldn't, except from putting her heart in jeopardy yet again from having an intimate dinner for two with him.

'I'll pick you up at seven,' he suggested, trying to sound light, when the weight of the consequences weighed a ton. Had he just overstepped the boundaries of where friendship ended and the possibility of romance began? Of course he had. He knew this, and yet he wasn't prepared to unwind the predicament he'd put himself in. Put both of them in.

Her acceptance without hesitation preyed on him as she smiled and left the theatre. He watched her walk away, the sunlight casting a glow on her silky strawberry blonde hair, feeling his heart ache just looking at her.

'Huntly,' Niall said to him. 'The radio show want to know if we can take part in their live chat show rather than a recorded interview.'

'Yes, that suits me,' Huntly replied.

From the office he heard Niall confirm that they'd take part in the interview during the live show. They'd been interviewed before, and it had gone well, so the host was keen to invite them on to talk about the new play that was part of their autumn and winter schedule.

There was nothing they needed to prepare as they were both capable of discussing their theatre business, especially as they had Mari's new play to chat about as a hot topic. He could sense the momentum building. Bringing Mari into their dramatic world was a great move. The new play had huge potential to be one of their biggest successes.

But what about Mari and him? Where should he draw the line between business and romance? He was already coming close to breaking his own rule of not becoming romantically involved with anyone he worked with. And yet, that rogue element in him, the fire that made him forge on when others might forgo challenges, burned bright in his heart for Mari.

No one watching Mari walk calmly away from the theatre in the lovely glow of the sunlight would guess how her heart beat with excitement. Dinner with Huntly at his house. Part of her wanted to enjoy seeing his lovely garden while the flowers were still in bloom. A cold spell could nip their beauty in the bud.

The weather this time of year was particularly unpredictable, though not as fickle as her feelings for Huntly.

On one level, she'd found him attractive since the first moment she'd seen him. But she'd forced herself to be sensible. She really didn't want to become romantically involved with anyone when she was trying to forge a new life for herself in Edinburgh. Plans and practicality clashed. She'd tried to keep her options for her career open. But meeting Huntly threw her senses to the wind.

Shaking her doubts and daydreams from her thoughts, she decided to go back to her flat and get some writing done before it was time to get dressed for dinner.

Sitting with her laptop near the window, she saw the sunlight slowly fade to a dusky amber and then deepen towards a gorgeous golden hour glow.

She'd surprised herself with her ability to become steeped in her story, working on her play. The heightened feelings from all that had happened recently seemed to have helped with her creativity rather than hindered it.

Closing her laptop, she got dressed for dinner, deciding that if she was going to be pottering around in his garden in the evening, a flimsy dress wasn't the right outfit to wear. Instead she put on a pair of burgundy velvet trousers, low heel black shoes, and a soft pastel pink jumper that helped give her pale complexion a rosy glow.

Brushing her hair smooth and silky, she wore subtle but flattering makeup, including a deep rose lipstick.

Her tweed jacket and bag were ready to pick up when Huntly arrived.

Despite peeking out the window every few minutes as seven o'clock approached, she missed seeing him drive up in his expensive silver car, and jumped when he rang the doorbell.

Grabbing her things, she turned the lights off and opened the door to find him standing there smiling down at her. Wearing a light blue shirt that made his eyes look even more like the colour of sapphires, formal dark trousers and a matching waistcoat, he was an assault on her heart.

'Ready to go?' His deep voice resonated in the calm night air.

'Yes,' she said lightly, smiling to hide her feelings for him.

He led her down to his car that was parked outside the closed craft shop. On such a lovely evening, the eateries were alive with social activity, but she was happy to be whisked away in Huntly's expensive car.

Neither of them noticed the black cat with green eyes sitting in the shadowed doorway of the old–fashioned shop watching them leave. A lantern light glowed from inside the shop. They didn't see that either. Then Spindle's sleek outline disappeared into the night. And the light in the shop flickered out.

Settling back in her seat, Mari gazed out the window as Huntly drove them through the heart of Edinburgh.

'I love the feel of the city at night,' she said.

'So do I. Edinburgh looks gorgeous in the autumn, and there's a richness to the evenings at this time of year. Winters are wonderful too. I remember one time it snowed in autumn, when the leaves on the trees were bronze and gold, but gilded with snow, sparkling like something out of a fairytale.'

'That sounds magical,' she said with a sigh.

'Maybe it'll snow in late autumn this year.'

'I wish.'

Huntly drove on, cutting through the heart of the city and headed towards his house, a traditional mansion surrounded by a garden with trees. Solar lights edged the pathway leading up to the house. The trees provided privacy around the edge of the property, many of them evergreens that would retain the density of their branches even in the heart of winter. Flower beds with an array of blooms, particularly roses, looked lovely.

He pulled up outside the front entrance and they got out of the car.

Huntly opened the boot and lifted out the two bags of fresh groceries he'd brought with him to make their dinner.

Mari stood for a moment and breathed in the heady scent of the greenery and flowers, and the potential that the night ahead held for both of them.

CHAPTER FOURTEEN

Huntly's house had a sense of drama to it, Mari thought on first impression when he led them inside the hallway and turned on the lights.

Lantern lights illuminated the hallway, sparkling like pendants from silvery fittings. The ceiling lanterns, in white and silver castings, were the main theme throughout the house as far as she could see. Varying in modern vintage styles.

Framed posters of past plays and shows from his theatre hung on the walls, and she wondered if her play would ever be hung there too.

A burgundy carpeted staircase led to the first floor, and the same carpet acted as a runner from the hallway off to the spacious rooms on either side of the hall, and deeper into the property where she followed him through to the kitchen.

The traditional house had that silence she so appreciated in her flat.

'Make yourself at home,' Huntly said, unpacking the groceries.

Excited to be there, she did feel at home in this welcoming house.

The kitchen felt like the hub of the house, beautifully kitted out with pale blue units that matched the walls, creating an airy atmosphere. A traditional dresser with plates, cups and ceramic teapots, and a sturdy wooden table and chairs, added to the homely quality.

But it had an extra element, a glass extension along one wall with a view of the back garden. The lawn and flower beds were lit with little solar lights, and the trees around the edges created a niche that she wanted to step out into.

Huntly fired up the professional level stove. 'Fish and chips sound okay to you?'

Mari smiled at him. 'Perfect.'

The impromptu dinner invitation made him opt for one of his tasty favourites.

'Have a wander around,' he encouraged her, gesturing through to the other rooms and the garden. 'There's a collection of plays and other books about the theatre in the living room that might interest you while I rustle up dinner.'

Huntly started to work efficiently, preparing everything with practised ease. He washed and peeled the potatoes, cut them into chips and parboiled them, then prepared the white fillets of fish and mixed the batter.

Mari wandered through to the living room and saw a bookshelf filled with a selection of titles. She picked one up and flicked through it, then put it back carefully. It looked like an original copy of a treasured classic. Eyeing another one that interested her, she read through part of it and then replaced it.

The room itself had a theatrical quality with an oil painting above the fireplace depicting Edinburgh at night from yesteryear. This traditional painting was offset with a light watercolour of his theatre's exterior awash with vibrancy. Perhaps he'd have a new painting added now that the lights adorned the theatre.

A scattering of framed character pen and wash artwork completed the theatrical theme of the decor.

After the busy day she'd had, the comfortable cream couch looked inviting to flop down on. She noted that the cushion covers were quilted, reminiscent of some that Ivy sold. A cosy throw was folded on the back of the couch, and she pictured snuggling down for a relaxing evening watching the wall–mounted television, selecting a film from Huntly's substantial collection.

A classic baby grand piano faced outward from one of the far corners, and in her mind she rewound the song she'd heard him play for her at the theatre. She imagined the room with its high ceiling would help the sound to resonate.

Sheet music was set up on the piano and she went over to take a peek at what he'd last been playing, intrigued to see that it was a romantic rhapsody.

The large lid of the piano was closed to prevent dust from accumulating inside it, as was the key lid.

Patio doors opened out on to the front garden. She clicked them open and peered out. The scent of the roses and gardenia from the garden mingled with the heady fragrance of the greenery and trees. Stepping outside, she meandered around feeling as if she was in a magical garden, and gazed up at the vast night sky arching above her, bright with twinkling stars.

One of her plays had a garden scene like this, and she pictured how the scenery would be portrayed if her romantic drama was performed on stage.

Blinking out of her deep thoughts, she went back inside the living room.

Full, plush creamy gold coloured carpeting added to the quietude, and it was only when she stepped on to the polished wooden floor leading through to another room that she heard her heels make a sound.

The second room was clearly Huntly's study where an antique desk and chair were set near the window. His computer and other items sat on the clutter–free desk.

The decor was darker in tone, creating a depth to his business world, as opposed to the lightness of the kitchen and bright tones of the theatrical style living room. The only nod to entertainment was the turntable set up to play his collection of vinyl records.

Every piece of his home told her something about Huntly, and as if creating the facets of a character from her plays, she was assembling the different traits that made him all the more intriguing to her.

The aroma of dinner cooking wafted through, enticing her back to the kitchen, but as she turned to leave, she noticed something that made her pause. A copy of her play, printed out like those she'd seen passed around in the theatre, sat on a table.

Seeing the title and her name on the play caused a wave of excitement to wash over her.

'Do you want wine or tea with your fish and chips?' Huntly called through from the kitchen.

She stepped up her pace and walked through to find that he was cooking the battered fish in a deep pan of hot oil and that the chips he'd made were keeping warm in the glass–fronted oven.

'Tea, and can I help to make it?' The kettle sounded as if it was nearly boiled.

Huntly took her up on her offer, but it was clear that he didn't need any assistance. Like a professional chef, he had everything sizzling, set and ready to serve as soon as the fish was cooked.

At the side of the sink was the dish he'd used to mix the batter. A plate retained a dusting of the flour mix he'd dipped the two pieces of fish in before coating them in batter.

White dinner plates and silverware like those in his turret were set on the table.

The scent of freshly cut wedges of lemon and minted garden peas mingled with the delicious aroma of the fish and chips.

Finding her way easily around his kitchen, she washed her hands and started to make the tea, filling one of the teapots and placing it on the table so they could top up their cups.

'Could you put the bread out,' he said, serving up the fish and chips that were cooked to a crisp and golden perfection.

Mari put slices of fresh bread on a plate and set it on the table along with the butter dish.

'This is a feast,' she said.

Huntly smiled. 'It's a tasty dinner to rustle up.' He added vinegar and a sprinkling of salt. Then he held up a jar. 'Pickled onions?'

'Yes, please.' She sat down at the table as he placed their plates down.

Fish, chips, peas and pickles along with a scoop of tomato sauce, tempted her taste buds.

Huntly buttered a slice of bread. 'Did you have a peek at the garden?'

'Yes, it's lovely and the scent from the flowers is gorgeous. And you have a beautiful house.'

'I'm fortunate to have a home like this. I really do need to find more time to relax here.'

'By the sounds of your schedule, your life is going to become even busier at the theatre with the new shows,' she said, wondering how he would manage this.

He sighed heavily. 'I'm hoping that once the dress rehearsals are done and the shows, including your play, are up and running, I'll have more time to myself, to potter around the garden, even in the colder months. I love the winter flowers, camellia, hellebore, daphne, clematis, pansies and jasmine.'

'A winter flowering garden sounds magical.'

'It is. As is the garden in the autumn. Though I'm so busy with the theatre.'

'When do the dress rehearsals start?'

'Tomorrow morning, for one of the other shows that we're launching after your play. Then it's the dress rehearsal the following day for our other drama.'

'Not much time for pottering in your garden,' she mumbled, eating one of the chips.

Huntly cut into the crisp batter on his fish. 'Not much time for anything.' Including nights like this with Mari he thought.

Mari helped herself to a slice of bread and butter. 'I'm excited to see the other new shows.'

'I think you'll enjoy them and you'll have the best seats in the house of course,' he said, smiling at her.

'Will you be there?'

He nodded. 'Me, Niall, our various directors, and others involved in the shows. I like to see how the audiences react, and there's nothing better than to be part of the audience.'

She tucked into her dinner as Huntly talked about the opening nights.

'There are the after show parties at the theatre. They're great fun. We usually celebrate backstage, and sometimes head out to a dance venue. You'll be invited to all of these. So be prepared to have your glad rags ready to party.'

'I will.'

'Sometimes we have a theme, and everyone dresses to impress in whatever style we select. It's not fancy dress, more thematic. I've heard Art Deco being mentioned this year.'

'I saw a gorgeous gold Art Deco style dress hanging up on one of the rails in wardrobe. I'm not hinting that I want to borrow it.'

'Borrow whatever you want, unless it's part of the show's actual costumes,' he said.

'I don't know that I'm the glitzy gold dress type. In my mind it sounds wonderful. But I think you need a certain pizzazz to carry off something like that.'

'You've got pizzazz galore. Wear it. Talk to Heather. She'll tell you if it's earmarked as a costume or up for grabs.'

'I might at least try it on the next time I'm at the theatre.'

'Make sure to take a picture for your archives,' he reminded her.

'I've started taking more photos of my knitting, and my flat, and I'm eager to see the pictures in the newspaper tomorrow of us all outside the theatre.'

'You saw the lights during the day, but when I left the theatre this evening, it was aglow. You'll probably see it tomorrow evening, or soon. When I'm not tempting you away with my homemade fish and chips.'

She pointed her cutlery at her dinner. 'I was going to give this a perfect ten out of ten, but...'

Huntly looked over at her. 'What does it score?'

'Eleven.'

He laughed, and they continued to enjoy their meal and each other's company.

She declined his offer of pudding. He hadn't made any, but he offered her ice cream or a slice of fruit cake.

'No, I couldn't manage anything else,' she said.

'Not even a chocolate mint?' He had a box of luxury chocolate mints to tempt her with.

'I could probably manage a chocolate mint or two.' She helped herself to two and ate them while finishing her tea.

Huntly joined her.

When they'd finished their dinner, he opened the door of the glass extension and invited her outside.

'It's quite a mild evening,' he said, breathing in the calm night air. 'Would you like a brief tour?'

'Yes.' She followed him out to the garden.

Huntly turned on the patio twinkle lights and showed her around the back garden. 'I'd like to extend the lawn down to the trees. I'll tackle that in the spring, along with adding more roses and a herb garden. I've got a few potted herbs, but I'd like more for my cooking.'

'Is that a summerhouse?' She walked towards the structure that was in partial shadow.

'It's actually a winterhouse. Built to be a cosy haven during the colder months. There's insulation and a heater. I added that last year and it was lovely at Christmastime and especially when it was snowing. But I used it in the summer too.'

He turned a lantern on outside the front door of the sturdily build wooden structure, like a large shed. She went to peer in one of the windows, but he opened the door and lit a lantern inside.

Mari stepped in. It had two comfy wooden chairs with cushions, a table that could double as a desk, and a rug on the floor.

'This feels like it would be cosy on cold days,' said Mari.

'It is, and days when it rains.'

Huntly went to turn the lantern off as Mari stepped outside, and their bodies clashed in the close proximity of the winterhouse.

His handsome face was lit by the glow of the lantern, and his apology was swift. 'Sorry, my fault.' He stepped aside and let her leave.

Although she'd felt her heart react to him during dinner, she'd enjoyed their meal and their light chatter, and it sort of took the edge off the depths of the attraction she felt for him.

She knew she was playing with fire accepting his offer of dinner at his house, but like a moth to the flame, she hadn't resisted.

Walking back up to the house she was grateful for the pockets of light and shade in the garden as it shielded the rosy blush that had formed across her cheeks.

Huntly gestured to the front garden, and instead of going back into the kitchen, she let him lead her to the front of the house where she admired the profusion of roses and other florals.

'We can go back in through the living room,' he said, opening the glass doors.

They went into the living room.

'I noticed you have a piano like the one in the theatre,' she said.

Huntly nodded. 'I can't remember the last time I played it or what I played.'

'I had a nosy at the sheet of music,' she confessed. 'It was a rhapsody.'

'Oh, yes, a favourite of mine,' he said, remembering it now. 'It was a warm summer evening, so that was almost a season ago.'

Mari gave him an encouraging look.

Huntly smiled. 'Is that a will you play something look?'

'It is,' she said.

He lifted up the large lid of the piano so that the sound could filter out, and then sat down on the stool, opened the key lid and began to play the rhapsody.

Mari sat down on the couch listening to the rich tones of the music fill the room and resonate as she'd imagined. The sound was far more concentrated, confined to the smaller room rather than the theatre, but there was a grandeur to the classical piece of music that stirred her to the core.

When he finished she applauded. 'That was marvellous, even better than when I heard you play the new song in the theatre.'

'The rhapsody is a piece I've played for years, so I'm familiar with it. The composer's song is new to me. I can read music, but I'm more sure of the rhapsody.'

She understood, but was still enamoured by his playing.

Huntly updated her on the composer's progress of recording the new song. 'He's probably still working in the recording studio. We're paying for the session, the hire of the studio, so he can record the song. He's playing each instrument himself and recording each piece separately. Then the tracks will be mixed to become the finished song.'

Mari was fascinated to hear how the song was created in the recording studio. 'He must be talented to play several instruments.'

Huntly agreed. 'Piano, violin, harp and guitar are the main instruments.'

Mari frowned. 'Does that mean the composer can't perform the song live in the theatre.'

'That's right. I suppose he could play it on the piano with his own backing tracks as accompaniment. Niall mentioned this because he wondered if we should have a special recital one afternoon at the theatre of the play's theme song.'

'You could play piano and Niall could play guitar. The composer could then play the harp or violin, and get one other musician to play whatever was left.'

Huntly took a moment to consider Mari's suggestion. 'That's a great idea, and it would be a one–off performance. It would promote the play and the song.'

'Win–win,' said Mari.

'I'll run this idea by them tomorrow,' he said, smiling at her.

He stood up and closed the lids again on the piano and put the sheet music away.

'Would you like another cup of tea?' he offered, extending their evening.

It was getting late, but Mari was in no hurry to go. 'Yes, thanks.'

She followed him through to the kitchen, and while he made the tea they chatted about the play, the publicity and about the forthcoming story in the next day's newspaper.

'Be prepared for more interest in you,' he said. 'Expect calls from other directors, people in the theatre business, and news journalists wanting to interview you for their publications.'

'Should I accept the interviews?'

'Yes.'

'Would you and Niall be part of them?'

He nodded as he poured their tea. 'But some of them will just want to talk to you.'

Mari tried to look calm, but whenever being in the limelight cropped up, she felt anxious. And yet she knew she needed to be part of the publicity process.

Huntly handed her a cup of tea and they sat again in the kitchen, chatting, unaware of the time and how late it was when Mari finally decided she should go home.

'We've let the time get away from us again,' he admitted, flicking some of the lights off in the kitchen until there was only the soft glow from a couple of spotlights.

Mari had hung her bag on the back of a kitchen chair, and as she went to unhook it, Huntly stepped over to pick it up for her, and he found himself pressed against her for a moment.

It was a moment that lingered, as neither of them immediately stepped back.

She gazed up at him, seeing his lips barely a breath away, those firm, sensual lips that made her heartbeat soar.

And in the cosy closeness of the kitchen, so late at night, he leaned down to kiss her, and then stopped a fraction from pressing his lips on hers.

'I'm sorry, Mari.' He stepped back and ran a hand through the front of his hair, as if to clear his senses. 'I didn't invite you to have dinner tonight to...well, put you in a compromising situation.'

She believed him. 'It's okay,' she said, hearing the tension in her voice. 'We're both just...' What? She didn't have the words to describe the truth without letting him know how deeply he affected her.

Huntly picked up his car keys. 'I'll drive you home.' He tried to sound gentle and calm, but she could sense the tension in him.

As he led her out to the car, he felt disappointed in himself. And yet, Mari hadn't challenged him for almost overstepping the boundaries of friendship. Her attitude helped smooth things over.

Driving away from the house, Mari glanced in the mirror, wondering if she'd ever be there with Huntly again.

CHAPTER FIFTEEN

Morning sunlight shone in the clear, autumn sky as Mari walked along the cobbled street reading the newspaper. She'd bought a copy from the grocery shop, and was eager to see if the theatre story was in it.

And there it was. The main picture showed her standing outside the theatre with Huntly and the others. Huntly stood next to her and she couldn't help noticing how tall he was. She barely came up to his shoulders. But it was a photo that captured the happiness of them all together, with the theatre's new lights on display.

She read the headline:

New playwright's drama launches theatre's autumn entertainment.

Walking on towards Ivy's shop, she intended showing her the story, excited to share it with her. It crossed her mind to phone Huntly and tell him they were featured in the paper, but their previous night's dilemma still stung. He was bound to read this for himself, and she didn't want him to think she was using it as an excuse to call him.

The beautiful bright morning had a warmth to it, not even a breeze strong enough to cause the bunting outside the craft shop to flutter.

Mari went inside, still holding the newspaper open and walked up to the counter where Ivy was adding the knitting needles that had arrived that morning to the theatre's knitted cat bags.

'There's a story in today's paper about the theatre,' Mari said, hearing the excitement in her voice.

Ivy dropped everything she was doing. 'Let me have a look.'

They stood together reading the feature, commenting about the pictures and the editorial.

'The theatre looks great with the new lights up,' Ivy remarked. 'And Huntly seems pleased to be standing next to you.'

'He does.' Mari sounded wistful.

'Is there something amiss?' said Ivy, picking up on Mari's tone.

'I had dinner with him at his house last night...' Mari revealed the details, and the outcome. 'He nearly kissed me. And I almost let him.'

'Oh, that's so romantic.'

'We'd both agreed not to become romantically involved. We're in the thick of everything with the theatre, launching the new play.' Mari sighed as if it was exhausting. And she did feel emotionally exhausted from trying to juggle her career taking off and her feelings for Huntly.

'There's never the right time when it comes to falling in love,' Ivy said wisely. 'If I'd dithered around when Bob proposed, I shudder to think that I could've ruined our chances of happiness.'

Mari shook her head. 'We've agreed to put romance on the back burner.' She told Ivy how he'd driven her home, walked her to the front door of her flat and they chatted for a few minutes, sealing the deal that they'd both rein in romance and put their relationship back on a friendly basis.

'At least you're not saying never,' said Ivy, sounding hopeful.

'It's never for now, and for the foreseeable future.'

'That's a wee shame,' Ivy told her truthfully. 'But you'll know what's right for you. Everyone's romance is different. Bob and I suit each other. We have lots in common and lots not. He's a baker. I don't bake, but I chat to him about his new recipes. I knit and sew. Bob doesn't, but he helps me select the fabrics and stacks the shelves when we restock at night. We share our business interests and our home life. It works, but your talent as a playwright could really soar.'

'I feel I can't take on any more drama in my life right now. I've enough with trying to write new plays. But Huntly is a magnet for drama.'

Ivy nodded. 'I have my own craft shop business. But I don't think I could've done what you did, giving up a reliable career in accounts to hang your hopes and dreams to a star, and take a huge leap to move to Edinburgh. That takes guts and hard work.'

Mari felt a little bit tearful, knowing how hard it had been, but she was now starting to gain the benefits.

'So if you think you can't add romance with Huntly, then don't. Take things easy as you say,' said Ivy. 'Huntly has a reputation for being unlucky in love. Remember, his last relationship ended in a blaze of verbal fireworks outside his theatre.'

Mari had taken that into account.

Ivy brightened and tapped the newspaper. 'But this is a story that makes you shine. I'm thrilled for you.'

Bob came bustling in, armed with tasty treats for his wife's morning break, and a copy of the newspaper tucked under his arm.

'I see you're infamous the day, lass,' Bob said to Mari.

'You've read the paper?' Mari surmised.

'Oh, aye,' Bob confirmed with a grin. 'Handsome Huntly looked fair chuffed with himself standing next to you in the photie.'

Bob's cheery attitude lifted the mood.

They chatted about her having dinner at Huntly's house, and how beautiful the house was.

'What did Huntly cook for you?' Bob was keen to know.

'Fish and chips. He cooked them from scratch,' said Mari. 'And they were delicious.'

Bob rubbed his hands together. 'It's put me in the notion for a fish supper for our dinner tonight.' He grinned at Ivy. 'How about I rustle that up for us this evening.'

'Oooh, tasty,' Ivy said, sounding enthusiastic. 'Bob's the chef in our wee hoose.'

'Did you help Huntly cook the fish supper?' Bob wanted to know more details. Anything cooking or baking related was of interest to him.

'No, he encouraged me to have a look around his house,' said Mari. 'He was happy to let me nosy at the living room, his study, and I had a walk outside in the garden. It's a gorgeous house and garden.'

'It sounds like Huntly's smitten if you ask me,' Bob announced, sounding sure of himself.

Ivy nipped his hopes of a romance between Mari and Huntly in the bud. 'They're taking things back to being friendly while they're in the whirlwind of getting the autumn and winter shows ready for the theatre.'

Bob sucked in a mouthful of air. 'Oooh, that's a gamble, lass,' he warned Mari. 'But you're a feisty one, so I'm sure you know what's right for you.'

Ivy peered into the two paper bags of cakes and buns he'd brought. 'There are some tasty treats in there this morning.' She smiled at Mari. 'I'll put the kettle on for tea and we'll have a wee celebration for you being in the paper, and finding success with your play.'

While the kettle boiled, Ivy's phone started to ping with messages, as did the computer screen behind the counter.

Bob took over making the tea while Ivy checked the influx of messages. She blinked after reading through them. 'Mari!' she said. 'Take a look at these. Lots of folk are wanting to order the theatre's knitted cat pattern.'

'What?' Mari peered at the messages, skim-reading them. 'They're saying they saw it in the paper.'

'You were holding the knitted cat when you were standing beside the actor.'

'Yes, Andy had fluffy and I had the knitted cat.' She checked the newspaper editorial. 'Oh, dear. I never read the caption under the photo. It says: *Knit your own cat*. And mentions that the kit is for sale in the theatre, contents supplied by you, Ivy, and that I designed it specially for the play.'

'Well, you did,' Ivy told her.

'Yes, but...look at all these orders. People want to knit the cat even before they've seen the play.'

'That's a good sort of chaos,' Bob called through to them as he made the tea and set a selection of cakes and buns on a plate.

Ivy shrugged happily. 'I ordered a load of the knitting needles.' Then she gestured to her stock of yarn on the shelves. 'And I've plenty of yarn. We'd just need to print out more copies of the pattern and the wee picture of the finished knitted cat. And Bob's your uncle!' Ivy concluded with a smile.

'Or in your case, your husband,' Bob chipped–in cheerily, carrying a tray with the tea and treats through and putting it down on the counter.

Mari had planned a calmer morning upstairs in her flat, reading the newspaper feature, and then getting on with her writing. But now her day had become crazy busy. So the last thing she needed was an urgent phone call from Huntly.

'Are you busy?' Huntly's tone was tense.

'Is this about the story in the newspaper?' said Mari.

'Yes and no,' he replied.

That was enough for Mari. 'I'm on my way.'

Grabbing a sticky bun and slurping down mouthfuls of her tea, Mari got ready to run. She shrugged her bag up on to her shoulder and rolled up the newspaper like a baton. 'Thanks for the celebration, but I have to dash. I'll call you later, Ivy.'

'No worries, Mari,' Ivy called after her, intending to enjoy a quick cuppa with Bob, but then she had to cut that short as two customers came in to buy the cat pattern.

Bob gave Ivy a squeeze and a cuddle. 'I'll see you later. And I'll organise what we need for our fish and chips dinner.'

Mari walked hurriedly up to the theatre. A car was parked nearby.

Huntly was outside the theatre helping the composer carry in a harp.

'I'll be with you in a minute,' Huntly called to Mari, walking into the theatre lugging his end of the harp.

'*And so it begins*,' Mari muttered to herself, following them into the foyer.

Niall called over to her from the office doorway. 'Do you know when the cats are arriving?' There was a mild hint of panic in his voice.

Rightly presuming Niall was referring to the pattern kits, she smiled calmly. 'Ivy is adding the knitting needles to the kits, so I'm sure they'll be delivered today.'

The relief showed on Niall's face and he disappeared into the office.

Mari decided to take the lesser of two stressful encounters and followed harp–carrying Huntly into the auditorium.

Huntly and the composer were already halfway down the centre aisle heading for a storeroom backstage while the dress rehearsal of one of their new shows was in full flow.

Seeing Huntly manoeuvre the instrument past some of the production staff, including the show's director, Mari decided to wait where she was and watched part of the performance of the new vintage crime drama.

The scenery and lighting created a wild, windswept evening outdoors in the Scottish Highlands from yesteryear.

One of the lead actors wore the classic mackintosh from wardrobe that she'd imagined a detective character might wear.

His Scottish voice rang out eloquently from the stage. *'Unleash the hounds. Don't let him escape into the hills or we'll never find the scoundrel before nightfall.'*

An old–fashioned police officer stepped forward into the spotlight. *'Do you think the woman is still alive, Detective?'*

'We have to hope,' the detective replied. *'I promised her I'd protect her. But she won't survive a night outdoors in the wilds of Scotland without warmth or shelter.'*

The police officer showed his concern, and the stage lighting changed to create a forthcoming storm effect. *'A storm is imminent, sir. Look at those dark, fast–moving clouds sweeping in. You could get caught in the downpour.'*

The detective turned the collar of his coat up and faced stage left. *'I'll take my chances with the elements. But we must make haste.'* He strode off as a flash of lightning ripped across the stage.

Dramatic music filled the minimal gap for the scenery to be changed for the opening of the next act.

Mari found she'd become quickly engrossed in the romantic crime drama, and forgot about the real drama for a few moments, until she saw Huntly emerge from backstage and walk towards her, sans the harp and the composer.

'I'll explain everything in the office,' Huntly said in a hushed voice, ushering her away from even a peek at act two.

'That sounded great. I'd be interested in watching it,' said Mari.

'Your ticket will be put aside,' he promised.

They walked into the office to find Niall had gone.

Rather than complicate things, Mari let Huntly tell her why he'd called.

He picked up a copy of the paper that was folded open at the feature. 'What did you think when you read it?'

'It's excellent publicity,' she said, and then added Ivy's predicament.

'We've had people phoning to book tickets for your play, but some of them wanted to buy the cat pattern now.'

'Ivy will have a bundle of the kits ready later today,' she assured him.

Huntly sighed with relief. 'It's tricky. We don't want people disappointed before they've even seen the play. But that cat has certainly tweaked people's interest more than we'd anticipated. Even I'm now eyeing the kit and thinking, yes, that looks doable.'

Mari laughed.

'Okay, cat kits galore are due today,' Huntly said, starting to list off the things that needed dealt with. 'The composer worked late into the night at the recording studio to lay down all the tracks for the song. So that's done and mixed. He let me hear it, and it's a winner. I'll let you hear it later.'

'And the harp?' she prompted him.

'I told the composer about your idea for an afternoon recital at the theatre and he jumped at the chance. He's chosen to play the harp, and one of the session musicians at the recording studio is hired to play the violin.'

'And will you play the piano?'

'I will.'

'And now I'm having to practise the song on my guitar,' Niall added walking in on their conversation. He didn't seem at all confident.

'You're a wonderful guitar player,' Huntly bolstered him.

'I don't play classic songs, just popular tunes,' said Niall. He ran an anxious hand through his thick blond hair. 'Have you seen the sheet music? I'd have an easier time deciphering a secret code.'

'Oh, pluck up,' Huntly joked with him.

Niall's stern face broke into a grin. 'If I get my fingerpicking in a fankle, it'll be your fault, Huntly.'

'I'm in the same pickle, Niall,' the composer said, smiling as he walked in to join them. 'I've never played a harp live on stage in a theatre like this. I'm not sure how it'll sound.'

Mari surmised this was why the harp had been brought there for him to practice.

'Once the dress rehearsal is finished, you can have the stage to yourself,' Huntly told the composer.

And then Huntly introduced them.

'I feel I know you from reading your magnificent play,' the composer said, shaking hands with her.

'I love your song,' she told him.

Introductions made, Huntly put the kettle on to boil to make them all tea while he revealed his next issue. 'Press interest has soared. We usually send out a press release and photos to the papers, magazines, radio and others. It saves hassle. The press publicity is usually organised, but with us doing the magazine feature, then the story in today's paper, well...' Huntly took a deep breath and showed her the messages on his phone. 'We've been inundated with requests for interviews from other papers and the like.'

'Can't you just send them the press release and photos you'd intended?' said Mari.

'No, now they all want exclusives like the two we've done,' Huntly explained.

Peter popped into the office and spoke to the composer. 'I've made room for your harp backstage. You can come and practice while you're waiting on the rehearsal to finish.'

Smiling, the composer left with Peter, eager to get some practise in, even if it was backstage.

'When are you planning to have the afternoon recital?' said Mari.

Huntly started setting up the cups for tea. 'Before the radio interview and that's soon.'

'People are buying tickets already,' Niall told her. 'We pinned up a notice in the window, and many of them coming in to buy tickets for the shows have snapped up tickets for the afternoon recital as well.'

'That's fast,' said Mari.

'Yes, but, I've suggested to Niall that we invite some of the journalists to the recital to hear the new song and chat about your play,' said Huntly, pouring their tea and offering them a piece of shortbread from a tin.

They all took a piece. None of them had eaten breakfast as the morning had charged by.

'I suppose that would take care of dealing with the interview requests,' Niall agreed. 'But if I mess up my guitar playing, the critiques will be scathing.'

'You won't and they won't. We know most of them anyway. They're looking for an interesting story,' Huntly reasoned. 'Four musicians that have never played on stage together, playing totally different instruments, and performing a new song for the first time — that's an interesting story.' Huntly smiled. 'What could go wrong?' He bit into his shortbread.

Mari and Niall laughed, and ate their shortbread before they were tempted to give Huntly a list.

Bob bustled in carrying one of his large bakery trays. But it was piled with the cat kits, not cakes.

'Hello, folks,' said Bob. 'Ivy said there's a rush job on with these kits. I was up this way making my deliveries so...here you go. Round one.'

Grateful for the delivery, Huntly and Niall relieved him of the kits, ushering him through to the foyer where they unpacked them into the small shop that was set up beside the box office. Mari followed them through to help.

'That was a great story about you all in the paper this morning,' Bob told them. Then he grinned at Huntly. 'And I hope you know you're responsible for me having to cook homemade fish and chips for Ivy's dinner tonight. I hear your batter was tasty.'

Mari smiled tightly and tried not to look like she'd blabbed all about her dinner date with Huntly.

But Huntly seemed amused. 'I'll message you a copy of my recipe,' he said to Bob.

'Cheers!' Bob gave him the thumbs up.

Jon wandered in as Bob bounded out the theatre.

'How did your dinner go with Scarlet?' Huntly said to Jon while Niall arranged the piles of cat kits in the shop.

Jon looked his usual suave self. 'Wonderful.'

'Are you having dinner together again?' said Niall.

'We are,' Jon confirmed. 'But...dinner didn't go the way I thought it would.'

'What went wrong?' said Mari.

'Nothing,' said Jon. 'I thought there would be tension and trouble, but we had a lovely time together. It was quite...romantic. No drama, and in my world that's a novelty.'

'In my world too,' Huntly muttered.

Mari glanced at Huntly and nodded.

'So we're planning to take things nice and easy,' Jon explained. 'We'll have dinner again soon, but we have to work around Scarlet's theatrical schedule. She's due to go into full dress rehearsals with her director for her new show, and then she'll be on stage in the evenings during her performances.'

'That could work,' said Mari. 'Taking things slow, while working around your careers.'

Jon brightened, glad that Mari understood. 'Yes, that's what Scarlet and I think.' He paused thoughtfully. 'Scarlet says she's going to cook dinner for me one evening at her place, maybe after one of the show nights.'

'Scarlet is going to cook you dinner?' Niall was surprised.

'Yes, she's actually quite the homebody,' said Jon. 'Once you get to know her.'

'Well, I'm happy for you,' said Huntly.

Mari smiled and agreed.

'So, what's on our plates today?' said Jon.

'Well, you missed the harp harassment, the cat kit emergency orders, Sammy creating a thunderstorm on stage, Niall baulking at having to play classical guitar, Bob wants my recipe for fish batter, and we're a hot topic in one of the papers,' Huntly told Jon.

'Another normal day here at the theatre,' said Jon. 'Is the kettle on? I skipped breakfast.'

'Yes, I'll make us another round of tea,' said Huntly, leading the way into the office, scooping Mari along with them. 'And we've a tin of shortbread.'

'Great stuff,' said Jon, heading in to tackle whatever was on their schedule and read the news in the paper.

'This is wonderful publicity,' said Jon, sipping his tea to wash down the shortbread.

A message came through for Mari while they all chatted. She saw that it was from Scarlet:

Thanks, Mari, for letting the cat out of the bag about me liking Jon. We had dinner last night. Things look promising. And I love the knitted vest. Scarlet, x.

Without telling them, Mari smiled to herself and put her phone away again.

While she was in the office, Niall wanted her help with the accounts. It was another tea break task and she was happy to help, while Huntly and Jon discussed their plans for the launch of the play.

'Ticket sales have soared,' Huntly told Jon. 'And with this story in today's paper, they'll take another jump.'

'Scarlet was telling me that everyone in her circle is talking about Mari's new play,' said Jon. 'And wondering what she's working on next.'

Mari finished adjusting the figures on the accounts and saved the changes she'd made. 'I'm writing a romantic adventure, probably, or maybe something totally new. But definitely with an element of romance.'

'Nearly all of us are in the mood for romance these days,' said Jon, throwing a knowing look at Huntly. 'Isn't that right?'

'Indeed it is,' Huntly agreed, feeling his heart ache a little just seeing Mari there with them.

'Audiences love romance,' said Jon. 'Whether it's a play with drama, music, dancing or intrigue. So add romance galore,' he said to Mari.

She nodded. 'I'll do that.' If she had to put romance on hold in her real life, she was happy to write about it in her plays.

And so she did.

Over the next short while, as the dress rehearsals took over the theatre, she was able to snuggle in her bolthole and write.

Huntly kept his contact with Mari to a friendly but professional minimum, giving her time to sort out her own plans without him adding drama.

But he did miss her.

A rainy spell made Mari's flat feel cosy during the days when she sat by her window, writing, while listening to the comforting sound of the rain. Taking time out to concentrate on her plays showed her that her dreams of being a playwright suited her.

Teaching the knitting classes were a pleasant break from her writing, and it was handy just to pop down to the craft shop. The spindle work continued to be popular with the class, and the members had their second lesson, learning to ply the yarn they'd first spun.

Mari had finished Niall's jumper too and dropped it off at the theatre office one morning before getting on with her day. He'd been delighted with the wintry grey and white colours and the design. It fitted him well. Huntly had been working with one of the other directors backstage, discussing last minute plans for the launch of the new drama, so she hadn't seen him before she left.

But she was looking forward to attending the afternoon music recital, and although she'd been in her own little bubble of writing and some knitting, she knew that the excitement was building for the launch of her play. She could feel it in the air, even as she hurried in the rain under her umbrella, away from the theatre and back to her flat.

Nights felt as magical as ever, and sometimes she caught a glimpse of Spindle outside the old shop, and sensed him keeping a watchful eye on her. Maybe she'd never know his true story, or that of the elusive shop owner. But that was okay, she thought. She felt the magic of both, and the intrigue.

But she had come across something else. While reading another interview about the theatre, one she'd taken part in, having talked to the journalist over the phone, she noticed a snippet of information that interested her. The journalist had delved into the background of the theatre, and found out that there had been a show in the past involving a little silver star. The star still hung above the stage. The one she'd seen. And it was said to sometimes grant wishes. It was a nice fairytale she'd thought.

After making her dinner one evening, and then writing into the night, she gazed out at the view of the city. The rain had stopped and the air looked so clear that the stars appeared extra bright.

Tucked up in bed, she gazed out at the starlight, looking forward to hearing the new song played by Huntly and the others at the theatre the following afternoon. Huntly had sent her a copy of the composer's studio recording and it sounded great, but she was keen to hear the live rendition of the song.

Thinking about Huntly playing the piano for her at his house, she drifted off to sleep.

Huntly and Niall were working late at the theatre, setting up the stage ready for the afternoon recital.

'The harp looks fine stage right,' Huntly snapped at Niall. 'You'll play your guitar under the spotlight on the left. Sammy has set it up nicely. The violinist will sit nearer the composer. And I'll play the piano where it is.'

Huntly sounded grumpy. He'd heard it in himself. He attributed it to his hectic schedule, getting all the shows organised.

'What's got into you recently?' Niall challenged him. He agreed with the set up for the music. But Huntly was back to his old ways of being brusque. 'You'd left that blunt attitude behind you. Now it's back. What's wrong?'

'There's nothing wrong,' Huntly said bluntly.

Niall shook his head and started to switch the lights off on the stage.

Huntly turned the lights off in other parts of the theatre as they got ready to leave.

Deep down, Huntly sensed what was wrong. He missed Mari. It was as simple or as complicated as that.

Niall knew him better than Huntly imagined. 'You should call her.' His advice to Huntly hung in the air as he left the theatre to drive home.

'I'm sorry I was blunt, Niall,' Huntly called after him.

Niall raised his hand, assuring him it was fine. 'See you tomorrow. I've been practising my guitar. Be prepared to up your game on the piano.'

Huntly smiled, sensing everything was okay between them, and headed up to the turret to get some sleep.

Mari arrived at the theatre the following afternoon and sat in one of the seats near the front of the stage.

Huntly, Niall, the composer and the violinist were ready to play the new song. They'd all worn dark suits, shirts and ties, smartly dressed for the special performance.

A starlight sky sparkled as the stage backdrop, and twinkle lights and spotlights created a starry night atmosphere.

The publicity had sparked interest in attending and the theatre was busy. Journalists had turned up to hear the song and cover the story. The low buzz of chatter faded as the lights dimmed.

And the music began, filling the theatre with the melodic sounds of the play's theme song.

Mari felt the melody touch her heart, and seeing Huntly sitting at the piano playing so expertly filled her with joy. Niall performed well too. They all did. The sounds of the harp created accents to the song, along with the violin, but Mari couldn't help but admire Huntly playing the piano. He'd seen her in the audience and looked out at her, before concentrating on his playing.

Peter was filming the performance and they intended putting a video of it on the theatre's website.

Ivy had closed her shop for the afternoon and was there with Bob. Huntly had made sure they had tickets.

Heather was there too, as were others, including Jon and Andy.

When the song finished, the audience applauded and Mari looked around at all the delighted faces.

Then the composer played a solo piece on the harp that then led to the others joining in with a classic composition, one of the composer's other songs. Two more songs followed, including one where only Huntly and the composer played. Then Niall played a popular song on his guitar. The audience continued applauding as the performance ended, and wanted an encore of the theme song.

The foursome were happy to oblige, and Mari enjoyed the second performance as much as the first.

It was a truly successful event, and as the audience filtered out, Huntly headed over to talk to Mari, but got caught up in the congratulations from others. And then the journalists wanted quotes from him and the others to include in their news stories.

Huntly beckoned Mari to join them, and she did, giving comments to the journalists too.

As everyone finally left, a rehearsal for her play was scheduled for that evening.

Thinking he was encroaching on Mari's time unnecessarily, Jon assured her that she didn't need to stay and should go home and write or get some rest. 'But come to the full dress rehearsal. I'll call you.'

'I will,' she said. Seeing the lights, the costumes and the whole performance set her heart fluttering with the pre–show nerves Andy had mentioned to her.

As she headed out, Huntly hurried after her.

'Mari!'

She stopped and they spoke briefly.

'We've both been so busy lately, I feel I've hardly seen you,' said Huntly.

'You told me this would be a whirlwind, getting all the shows ready. We've both been busy.'

'Yes, but...' his words trailed off. She'd no idea how much he wanted to pull her close and tell her he'd missed her. Even though she was close by, it wasn't the same as before.

'Huntly,' Peter called to him. 'I need you to approve the video for the website. Do you want me to include the second performance of the song too?'

Smiling at Huntly, Mari walked away, leaving him to attend to the busy running of the theatre.

Andy ran around in costume backstage, carrying Fluffy and Tiddles, in a mild panic about the full dress rehearsal. Dashing into his dressing room, he checked his appearance in the mirror. His costume looked great.

He'd learned his lines. The cats were perfect foils for his performance, and the other actors were a delight to work with. But nerves came with the territory, he reminded himself. It kept his performances electric.

Hearing the sound check of the theme song, and the flashing light in his dressing room alerting him that he was due on stage, Andy straightened his shoulders under his dark blue tailcoat, looked at the double load of luck he had with two prop black cats, and strode out ready to perform.

Mari sat near the front row of seats, sandwiched between Jon and Niall. Huntly had been rushing around helping Sammy, advising on the sound level of the theme song.

The opening notes of the song had started when Huntly ran over to join Mari and the others. He had to sit on an aisle seat rather than his preferred place right next to her.

The atmospheric and exciting start of the play outshone his hopes, and he knew they had a success on their hands.

But his feelings for Mari tormented him in ways he'd never felt before. Stronger, deeper. It was an experience he wished he could cast aside, at least until the shows were launched. They'd gambled that Mari's play was the one to lead the charge of their new schedule. He was confident it would pay off well.

Tickets sales exceeded all their past box office records. The theatre was a success. His personal life was in tatters. He'd snookered himself with his own stupid rule of not mixing business and romance.

He could scrap it if he wanted, and he'd nearly scuppered it by almost kissing Mari when she'd been at his house. But he'd made such a song and dance about not becoming romantically involved with her.

Unravelling the emotional ropes that were binding him would be tricky. And the last thing he wanted was to play around with Mari's trust and feelings. He'd handled things badly. Now it was up to him to sort it out.

Mari was engrossed in the play, loving the actors' performances, and the look of the stage settings right down to the props including Fluffy and Tiddles. Glancing at Huntly, she noticed the tension in his profile, the muscles in his jaw clenched with...she wasn't sure. Vexation? Annoyance? Had he been fighting dragons again?

'This is outstanding,' Jon whispered to Mari.

'Yes,' she whispered.

The comment stretched to Niall and made its way to Huntly, and there were nods of great approval from them too.

So why was Huntly perturbed? Deciding she didn't want to ruin the play by trying to figure out what was up with him, she let herself relax and enjoyed the show.

Discussions backstage later were all positive. Everyone thought the play was more than ready to launch their new season.

Huntly was engrossed with crew and other actors while Mari chatted to Niall, Jon and Andy.

If any of them noticed Huntly being distant, they never mentioned it to her. And from the interactions, she was inclined to think that it was due to circumstances rather than choice on his part.

Leaving the theatre, Mari stood talking to Niall and Jon, and then walked back home. She told herself not to dwell on Huntly being out of sorts. The launch of her play was imminent.

Mari peered out the window of her flat. It was a clear, calm evening. Perfect for the opening night of her play. But she was far from calm. She'd changed her dress twice, deciding that she would wear a lovely marigold yellow tea dress, a vintage find that fitted her so well and was a nod to her full name.

For the opening night of her play, it seemed appropriate.

Jon had called her recently to attend the play's dress rehearsal, and she had enjoyed seeing the magnificent melee where last minute changes were made to the sets and the costumes. The dialogue remained unchanged, so she'd been able to watch the whirlwind whiz around her.

Now, it was the opening night.

Taking a deep breath, she looked at herself in the mirror. Her long–held dream was about to become real in the most extraordinary fictional setting.

Wearing a cream coat over her dress, she walked up to the theatre and her heart started to thunder with excitement when she saw it all lit up in the night and people heading inside to watch the play.

She could hear them chatter, looking forward to the show. Their smiles would be a memory she'd treasure.

No one recognised her as she joined in the flow of people heading into the foyer. And she preferred that.

The foyer was alight with laughter and excitement.

Huntly was standing near the door of the office with his back towards her. He wore a classic dark suit, and her heart reacted seeing him there. He suddenly glanced round, as if sensing she was there, and his face lit up with a smile that left her in no doubt that he was pleased to see her.

They walked towards each, and Huntly swept her into the office. They were alone, but she could hear the chatter of the audience in the foyer.

'Let me take your coat,' he said, relieving her of it and hanging it over one of the chairs. Her hair hung in soft waves around her shoulders. He took in how lovely she was. 'You look beautiful.'

He looked handsome in his suit, white shirt and silk tie. 'You're looking dapper.'

'Come on,' he said, sweeping her out of the office, through the foyer and into the auditorium. The seats were swiftly filling up. As they walked down the centre aisle she expected him to show her to her seat. Instead he continued on, taking her backstage where the excitement from the cast and crew was palpable.

Rushing around in organised chaos, getting ready for their opening night of the season, Mari loved having a peek behind the curtain of how a play was launched.

First night nerves were contagious, for Mari started to feel anxious about how her play would be received. But hugs and warm smiles from everyone from Heather to Peter and Jon soothed her trepidation.

'Andy wants to see you in his dressing room before he goes on,' Huntly said to Mari, leading her along the corridor.

Andy's dressing room door was open. The dressing table mirror, edged with lights, created a bright, warm glow that matched his smile when he saw her walk in.

That quicksilver movement took her aback as he got up from his chair and gave her a hug. 'This is it,' he gushed. And then tapped his heart. 'First night nerves. For you I suppose as well as me.'

'Yes, though I'm going to be sitting in the audience with Huntly and the others while you bring the play to life,' she said.

Andy clasped both her hands in his and gave them a reassuring squeeze. 'I've acted in various shows, but this play of yours is special.' His blue–green eyes were alight with energy.

Mari glanced to see if Huntly agreed, but he'd gone, and she could hear him chatting to Jon in the hallway about the after show party.

Andy was given his five minute alert, and Mari left him to get ready to go on stage.

Huntly whisked her along backstage. 'We'd better get to our seats. The show's about to start.'

'I'm more nervous than Andy,' she said as Huntly clasped her hand and led her through the busy backstage area and out front to their seats. Jon and Niall were already seated and nodded and smiled when she joined them.

Huntly was seated next to her this time.

'Is the theatre always this busy?' Mari glanced around. Every seat from the stalls to the balcony and dress circle were filled. She smiled when she saw that Ivy and Bob had been given tickets to the box seats with a great view of from high up at side of the stage. Dressed to the nines, they exchanged a quick nod and wave with Mari and Huntly.

'This evening's opening was a sell out,' Huntly whispered to her.

Then the lights dimmed, the chatter stopped, and the opening notes of the theme song wafted out over the audience, setting the atmosphere for the start of the play.

The depiction of the old–fashioned shop, aglow with lights at night, was wonderful. The evening backdrop created depth to the stage, and the starry sky effect was lovely.

Mari felt mesmerised by the atmosphere they'd created, and began getting wrapped up in the play, even though she'd written it.

The audience enjoyed the theme song, and then became engrossed in the intriguing story.

During the short interval, Huntly hurried Mari backstage again to experience being part of the production.

'This is wonderful,' Mari said gazing around her. 'What a world to be part of.'

'I love it. I've always loved the theatre,' he said.

As crew went by with a change of props, Huntly pressed himself against Mari to let them hurry on.

She felt the strong, lean strength of his body shield her, and a blush rose in her cheeks at the effect his closeness had on her.

For a moment she thought he would step back, but no. Huntly gazed down at her, still close enough to kiss her.

Although he resisted the temptation that took every ounce of his resolve, he didn't hide how he felt.

'I've missed you, Mari.' His rich, deep whisper sent her heartbeat soaring.

'I've missed you too,' she confessed. And in that unguarded moment, they both felt the intense spark of attraction ignite between them.

'Five minutes!' The call for the actors and crew interrupted their moment.

Would Huntly have kissed her? Would she have resisted?

She thought she knew the answers, and this would surely lead to risking her heart by falling in love with Huntly.

Joining the others in their seats again, Mari and Huntly watched the rest of the play, enjoying the drama and romance of it all, and the little bit of magic.

The audience seemed to love the lead character of Oglesby and his cat, Spindle. And during the interval, members of the audience had bought the kit from the theatre shop to knit their own cat.

'I hope you're attending the after show party,' Huntly murmured to Mari.

'I wouldn't miss it.' She wanted to experience every part of the theatre life with Huntly and the others.

Backstage after the successful show, the cast and crew partied into the night. Music played, and there was dancing, a buffet and refreshments, including champagne.

Huntly picked up two glasses of the bubbling champagne and handed one to Mari.

She held it up and they tipped their glasses in a cheers.

Mari smiled at Huntly and gazed around at the new friends, like a large boisterous family, that she'd made. 'Do you know what I like about this evening? Apart from the play being a success.'

Huntly shook his head. 'No, what?'

'That this is not over,' she said, her voice filled with excitement. 'It's the start of other nights like this. Of drama and fun, celebrating and partying after the shows. I'm looking forward to the opening nights of the other shows too. And to seeing Wil's dance performance.'

'It's a different world than the one you've been used to,' he said.

Mari nodded up at him. 'A world I could learn to love deeply.'

Huntly put their glasses aside and gently pulled her close. She didn't resist.

'Anyone else you could learn to love?' he said in a romantic whisper.

'I believe so,' she murmured, feeling his strength as he took her in his arms.

'I've been learning that since the day you first walked into the theatre,' he confessed. 'I've been fighting to suppress falling in love with you. Without success.'

'I've been falling in love with you too,' she whispered as others went by, smiling at them.

'I think I'm causing drama in your life again,' he said lightly.

'I could get used to that.'

'I wish with all my heart that you will.' As he said this, the silver star above the stage sparkled, catching both of their attention.

'I've a feeling our wishes will come true.'

Huntly nodded, and then leaned down and kissed her, again and again.

The reviews for her play were marvellous, spurring her on to write her new plays.

The opening nights for the other shows were as exciting as Mari's play. And the after show parties did have an Art Deco theme one evening.

After the party, she went up the theatre turret with Huntly.

He stood with his arms wrapped around her as she gazed out at the glittering lights of Edinburgh. The beautiful night sky twinkled with stars.

She wore the vintage gold dress from the theatre's wardrobe, and had danced the night away in shimmering style.

Huntly had another type of gold in mind, a ring, that he planned to surprise her with around Christmastime, when wishes were more likely to come true. He wished to spend the rest of his life with Mari, on a theatrical adventure together, but with cosy moments when all they wanted was to snuggle up close.

'Oh, look,' she said, gazing at a black cat sitting on a distant rooftop.

Huntly saw the cat too.

And then it disappeared into the night.

'I love that we have a little bit of magic in our world,' Mari said, leaning back against Huntly's strong chest.

Huntly gently swept her around until he was gazing down at her. 'I love more than anything that we found each other.'

'I do too, Huntly,' she murmured.

His firm lips kissed her and she felt her heart soar. And then they gazed out from the windows of the theatre turret making plans for their life together.

End

About the Author:

De-ann Black is a bestselling author, scriptwriter and former newspaper journalist. She has over 100 books published. Romance, thrillers, espionage novels, action adventure. And children's books (non-fiction rocket science books and children's fiction). She became an Amazon All-Star author in 2014 and 2015.

She previously worked as a full-time newspaper journalist for several years. She had her own weekly columns in the press. This included being a motoring correspondent where she got to test drive cars every week for the press for three years.

Before being asked to work for the press, De-ann worked in magazine editorial writing everything from fashion features to social news. She was the marketing editor of a glossy magazine.

She is also a professional artist and illustrator. Embroidery design, fabric design, dressmaking, sewing, knitting and fashion are part of her work.

Additionally, De-ann has always been interested in fitness, and was a fitness and bodybuilding champion, 100 metre runner and mountaineer. As a former N.A.B.B.A. Miss Scotland, she had a weekly fitness show on the radio that ran for over three years.

De-ann trained in Shukokai karate, boxing, kickboxing, Dayan Qigong and Jiu Jitsu. She is currently based in Scotland.

Her 16 colouring books are available in paperback, including her latest Summer Nature Colouring Book and Flower Nature Colouring Book.

Her latest embroidery pattern books include: Floral Garden Embroidery Patterns, Christmas & Winter Embroidery Patterns, Floral Spring Embroidery Patterns and Sea Theme Embroidery Patterns.

Website: Find out more at: www.de-annblack.com

Fabric, Wallpaper & Home Decor Collections:
De-ann's fabric designs and wallpaper collections, and home decor items, including her popular Scottish Garden Thistles patterns, are available from Spoonflower.
www.de-annblack.com/spoonflower

Also by De-ann Black (Romance, Action/Thrillers & Children's books). See her Amazon Author page or website for further details about her books, screenplays, illustrations, art, fabric designs and embroidery patterns.

Amazon Author page:
www.De-annBlack.com/Amazon

Romance books:

Music, Dance & Romance series:
1. The Sweetest Waltz
2. Knitting & Starlight

Snow Bells Haven series:
1. Snow Bells Christmas
2. Snow Bells Wedding
3. Love & Lyrics

Scottish Highlands & Island Romance series:
1. Scottish Island Knitting Bee
2. Scottish Island Fairytale Castle
3. Vintage Dress Shop on the Island
4. Fairytale Christmas on the Island

Scottish Loch Romance series:
1. Sewing & Mending Cottage
2. Scottish Loch Summer Romance
3. Sweet Music
4. Knitting Bee

Quilting Bee & Tea Shop series:
1. The Quilting Bee
2. The Tea Shop by the Sea
3. Embroidery Cottage
4. Knitting Shop by the Sea
5. Christmas Weddings

The Cure for Love Romance series:
1. The Cure for Love
2. The Cure for Love at Christmas

Sewing, Crafts & Quilting series:
1. The Sewing Bee
2. The Sewing Shop
3. Knitting Cottage (Scottish Highland romance)
4. Scottish Highlands Christmas Wedding

Cottages, Cakes & Crafts series:
1. The Flower Hunter's Cottage
2. The Sewing Bee by the Sea
3. The Beemaster's Cottage
4. The Chocolatier's Cottage
5. The Bookshop by the Seaside
6. The Dressmaker's Cottage

Scottish Chateau, Colouring & Crafts series:
1. Christmas Cake Chateau
2. Colouring Book Cottage

Summer Sewing Bee

Sewing, Knitting & Baking series:
1. The Tea Shop
2. The Sewing Bee & Afternoon Tea
3. The Christmas Knitting Bee
4. Champagne Chic Lemonade Money
5. The Vintage Sewing & Knitting Bee

Tea Dress Shop series:
1. The Tea Dress Shop At Christmas
2. The Fairytale Tea Dress Shop In Edinburgh
3. The Vintage Tea Dress Shop In Summer

The Tea Shop & Tearoom series:
1. The Christmas Tea Shop & Bakery
2. The Christmas Chocolatier
3. The Chocolate Cake Shop in New York at Christmas
4. The Bakery by the Seaside
5. Shed in the City

Christmas Romance series:
1. Christmas Romance in Paris
2. Christmas Romance in Scotland

Oops! I'm the Paparazzi series:
1. Oops! I'm the Paparazzi
2. Oops! I'm Up To Mischief
3. Oops! I'm the Paparazzi, Again

The Bitch-Proof Suit series:
1. The Bitch-Proof Suit
2. The Bitch-Proof Romance
3. The Bitch-Proof Bride
4. The Bitch-Proof Wedding

Heather Park: Regency Romance
Dublin Girl
Why Are All The Good Guys Total Monsters?
I'm Holding Out For A Vampire Boyfriend

Action/Thriller books:

Knight in Miami
Agency Agenda
Love Him Forever
Someone Worse
Electric Shadows
The Strife Of Riley
Shadows Of Murder
Cast a Dark Shadow

Children's books:

Faeriefied
Secondhand Spooks
Poison-Wynd
Wormhole Wynd
Science Fashion
School For Aliens

Colouring books:

Summer Nature
Flower Nature
Summer Garden
Spring Garden
Autumn Garden
Sea Dream
Festive Christmas
Christmas Garden
Christmas Theme
Flower Bee
Wild Garden
Faerie Garden Spring
Flower Hunter
Stargazer Space
Bee Garden
Scottish Garden
Seasons

Embroidery Design books:

Sea Theme Embroidery Patterns
Floral Garden Embroidery Patterns
Christmas & Winter Embroidery Patterns
Floral Spring Embroidery Patterns
Floral Nature Embroidery Designs
Scottish Garden Embroidery Designs

Printed in Great Britain
by Amazon